"You can't go down the aisle empty-handed and alone!"

"I know," Sophie said, holding out her arms for her son and pressing a kiss on his downy head.

If the guests at the Casson-Winter wedding happened to notice that the mother of the bride carried the bouquet intended for her daughter, they appeared not to care. They were too delighted by the sight of the bride carrying her infant son down the aisle to meet his father at the altar.

"It seemed the right thing to do," Sophie whispered when she reached Dominic's side. "Ryan should be part of this, not just an onlooker. We're a family, after all."

FROM HERE TO PATERNITY—romance novels that feature fantastic men who *eventually* make fabulous fathers. Some seek paternity, some have it thrust upon them, all will make it—whether they like it or not!

CATHERINE SPENCER, once an English teacher, fell into writing through eavesdropping on a conversation about Harlequin romances. Within two months she changed careers and sold her first book to Harlequin Mills & Boon in 1984. She moved to Canada from England thirty years ago and lives in Vancouver. She is married to a Canadian and has four grown children—two daughters and two sons— plus three dogs and a cat. In her spare time she plays the piano, collects antiques and grows tropical shrubs.

Books by Catherine Spencer

HARLEQUIN PRESENTS
1406—THE LOVING TOUCH
1587—NATURALLY LOVING
1682—ELEGANT BARBARIAN
1812—THAT MAN CALLAHAN!

HARLEQUIN ROMANCE
3138—WINTER ROSES
3348—LADY BE MINE
3365—SIMPLY THE BEST

CATHERINE SPENCER

Dominic's Child

Harlequin Books

TORONTO • NEW YORK • LONDON
AMSTERDAM • PARIS • SYDNEY • HAMBURG
STOCKHOLM • ATHENS • TOKYO • MILAN
MADRID • WARSAW • BUDAPEST • AUCKLAND

For Grace Green
with love and gratitude for her loyalty and support.

ISBN 0-373-11873-2

DOMINIC'S CHILD

First North American Publication 1997.

Copyright © 1996 by Kathy Garner.

Printed in U.S.A.

CHAPTER ONE

SOPHIE knew at once who it was rapping on her hotel room door in that imperious "Don't keep me waiting" manner, partly, of course, because the chief of police had forewarned her that Dominic Winter was en route to St. Julian, but also because there was in the summons nothing of the islanders' discreet *tap tap* that begged the favor of admittance.

Instead, this was the peremptory crack of bone on wood—the command of a superior being to one of lesser stature. If he'd bellowed, "Open the door, woman, and let me in!" his message could not have been clearer.

For all that she'd been expecting him, the proof of Dominic Winter's arrival had Sophie starting up out of the chair in a flurry of agitation. The sound of his knock seemed indecently loud somehow, and not at all fitting to the somber gravity of the occasion.

On her way to answer him, she made an unplanned stop before the mirror, though why she bothered escaped her. She knew her hair was perfectly in place, her attire as suitably subdued as could be achieved, given the sort of clothes she'd brought with her.

Perhaps it was because she needed to be sure that nothing in her face gave her away. Of course she was upset, saddened; under the circumstances, that was to be expected. But there was more. There'd always been something more where Dominic Winter was concerned, and that was what he must never suspect.

He strode into the room and, without the slightest concession to civil good manners, said in a tone as forbiddingly cold as his name, "Well, I hope you're happy with what you've done, Ms. Casson. My fiancée is dead and her parents are shattered."

"It was an accident," she heard herself reply defensively, and wondered why she didn't just set him straight and have done with it. Whatever other guilty secrets she harbored, culpability in Barbara's death was not among them. But one didn't launch into a diatribe about a dead woman's shortcomings, not to the man who'd hoped to marry her in another few months and certainly not within seconds of his arriving at the scene of her untimely demise. There would be opportunity enough for him to learn the details leading up to the accident later, when he'd recovered a little from the shock and from the draining exhaustion of travel.

If Sophie was prepared to show a little sensitivity, however, Dominic Winter was not. "You might call it an accident," he declared flatly, "but I've yet to be convinced that you aren't guilty of criminal negligence—in which case 'manslaughter' would be a more accurate term, or perhaps even 'murder'."

Sophie prided herself on being a capable, independent sort of woman. Going weak at the knees when someone tried to intimidate her simply wasn't her style. But she felt the blood drain from her face at his intimation. "Mr. Winter," she said, backing away from him unsteadily, "I was nowhere near Barbara when she died. In fact, I was completely unaware of her plans on Wednesday, and if you don't believe me then I suggest you check my alibi with Chief Inspector Montand, who is perfectly satisfied that I am in no way to blame for what happened to her."

"But I am not Chief Inspector Montand, Ms. Casson, and I do hold you to blame. You encouraged Barbara to come away with you. If you had not, she would be alive today."

What could she say that didn't sound like an excuse? Sophie bit her lip and turned toward the louvered doors that led to the balcony. Outside, the entire world seemed bent on the celebration of life. Everything, from the surf rolling rhythmically up the pale gold crescent of beach to the sultry sway of the coconut palms fringing the hotel grounds, seemed to echo the calypso beat of the ever-present steel band.

A scarlet hibiscus, shot full of burgundy fire from the sun, flamed next to an overpoweringly sweet-scented frangipani. Macaws perched on the backs of unoccupied sun chaises, brazenly flaunting their plumage.

But what she had found breathtakingly lovely only two days before struck Sophie now as obscene. How could there be death in the midst of such vibrant life? Tragedy did not marry easily with the carnival atmosphere that was St. Julian's stock-in-trade.

Closing her eyes, she struggled to find the words to ease Dominic Winter's pain. Because she knew he must be hurting, even though she'd noticed that he hadn't included himself among those shattered by Barbara's death. Or was that wishful thinking on her part? Would she have preferred him not to care?

Ashamed, she shut out the question just as, over the past ten weeks, she'd learned to shut out other inappropriate thoughts concerning this man. "I did not coerce Barbara into accompanying me, Mr. Winter," she said at last. "It was entirely her idea. In fact, she was so insistent she needed a change of scene to get her through the coming winter that if she hadn't come here with me, she'd undoubtedly have run off somewhere else."

"And you never thought to question the logic of that?"

"Why should I?" she cried, stung by his unremitting air of condemnation. "She was an adult, capable of making up her own mind, and I hardly knew her. If anyone should have recognized that she was...highly strung and wildly impetuous, it should have been you."

At that, the antagonism in his eyes faded somewhat and it occurred to Sophie that, for the only time in their acquaintance, he allowed her to see past the glower to the man inside. It also occurred to her how seldom she'd seen him smile, even in the early days of her association with Barbara when he'd presumably had every reason to be happy.

Sophie had met him in mid-September when she first began working at the Wexler estate, although perhaps "met" wasn't quite the word to describe his remote nod of acknowledgment when she had been introduced to him. Her first impression had been that he was a snob, the kind of man who found it beneath his dignity to treat an employee, whether his or someone else's, with the same respect he accorded to his own kind—even when, as in her case, the employee was a professional whose framed credentials attested to her expertise.

It was only later that she wondered if he made a particular point of maintaining a safe distance from her, a notion based more on feminine instinct than hard fact. Because, despite his apparent uninterest in her comings and goings, she'd several times caught him spying on her, even when she was at the far end of the property and about as far away from him as she could get. She'd look up and there he'd be at one of the long windows, or standing in the shade of the pergola that connected the Wexlers' handsome Georgian-style mansion to the rose gardens below the terrace.

Tall and authoritative, with astonishingly beautiful eyes that, depending on his mood, changed from rich deep jade to brilliant emerald ice, he was a man of presence and impossible to ignore. She found him disturbingly attractive yet formidably remote. She'd had no more idea what went on in that head of his than she could have unraveled the mystery of the sphinx. He had remained an enigma, despite her clandestine fascination with him—until now, when tragedy fractured his reserve and rendered him marginally more human.

"Barbara was like a child," he said, pacing back and forth across the tiled floor, "incapable of recognizing her own mortality. If she had told me ahead of time that she planned to sneak off with you, I'd have done my level best to stop her. And if I had not been able to succeed, I would have warned you to keep an eye on her. What I don't understand is why, if, as you claim, you hardly knew her, you decided to share a holiday with her."

"It was a last-minute thing," Sophie explained. "Usually, I travel with my friend, Elaine, but she came down with the chicken pox three days before we were due to fly down here. I happened to mention it to Barbara and she immediately offered to buy Elaine's ticket. I saw no reason to quarrel with that, especially since Elaine hadn't bothered to take out cancellation insurance and stood to lose rather a lot of money. But I did make it clear to Barbara that, once we arrived here, we'd go our separate ways for most of the time."

In less than a blink of his remarkable eyes, Dominic Winter's antagonism rolled back into place again, swathed in biting sarcasm. "In other words, Barbara became an inconvenience once she'd served the purpose of averting a financial loss for your friend. Allow me to say, Ms. Casson, that I am overwhelmed by so commendable an attitude. You're obviously all heart!"

"This is a working vacation for me, Mr. Winter. I couldn't afford the luxury of whiling away the time the way Barbara did. She understood that. If you choose to put the worst possible interpretation on my actions, there's little I can do about it."

"And even less that you care."

Oh, she cared, more than he could begin to guess! But she'd be damned if she'd let it show.

"Exactly," she retorted, then made matters worse by compounding the lie with an even greater untruth. "Your opinion of me matters not one iota and if that offends you, Mr. Winter, perhaps the knowledge that I'm singularly unimpressed by you, too, will even the score between us. I don't know quite how I expected you to behave today but if you'd shown a glimmer of compassion, I might have felt more kindly disposed to tolerate your insults. As it is, I can't quite shake the feeling that perhaps it was the thought of spending the rest of her life with you that drove Barbara to behave so rashly last Wednesday."

He had the kind of skin that glowed with sun-kissed radiance regardless of the season, but at her words his face grew bleached with shock. Equally appalled, Sophie stared at him, her gaze fused with his. The man was clearly in pain. What was it about him that compelled her to add to his misery?

She knew. She'd always known, right from the start: she was afraid of him.

She'd never dared explore the reasons. It was enough that, from the first moment she'd set eyes on him, she'd felt a stirring of hunger for something—some*one*—who wasn't hers to have. And so, out of self-defense, she'd manufactured a dislike of him, and it had worked well enough until now when his chilly reserve slipped.

Perhaps it was as well that, at that moment, the phone rang and provided them both with a distraction. Certainly she was glad of the excuse to turn away from him and busy herself picking up the receiver.

She listened a moment, murmured assent, then hung up. "That was Chief Inspector Montand," she told Dominic. "He's downstairs in the hotel foyer and would like to speak to us."

"Why us and not just me? If you're as blamelessly detached from this tragedy as you claim to be, what more can he possibly have to say to you?"

She shrugged, calling up that old, contrived antipathy to arm herself against him. It was easy enough to do, given his miserable attitude. "Ask him. I don't make the rules around here."

Yet she hated the way she sounded, so hard and uncaring, as though the fact that a young woman had died didn't matter as long as that person wasn't Sophie Casson.

It was almost comforting to hark back to Wednesday evening when the wreckage of the Laser had been found and the awful truth of Barbara's fate had begun to take shape. Sophie hadn't been flippant then. Her initial reaction of paralyzed disbelief had given way to near hysteria. It had taken a sedative prescribed by the hotel doctor to calm her down. Not even Dominic Winter could have doubted the sincerity of her distress that night.

Today, however, was a different matter. Contempt curling his incredibly sexy mouth, he flung wide the door and with an extravagantly courteous flourish ushered her into the hall outside. "Well, let's not keep the good inspector waiting, Ms. Casson. I'm sure you have more interesting things planned for this afternoon than rehashing the tedious minutiae of Barbara's death."

He is suffering, Sophie intoned silently. *Remember that and refuse to enter into hurtful mind games with him, no matter how much he goads you.*

Spine straight, head high, she swept ahead of him. Her navy-and-white-striped skirt fluttered around her calves in concealing folds but her low-backed white blouse with its halter neckline left her feeling woefully underdressed. She could almost feel Dominic's glare branding her bare shoulders with the stigmata of his disapproval.

She had reached the top of the sweeping staircase before he caught up with her. His hand cupped her elbow, a cool, impersonal touch that stemmed less from concern for her safe descent than from the habit of inbred good manners. She was tall, almost five feet eight inches, but beside him she felt small. Small and defiant, like a child trying to match wits with a punitive uncle. But she would not give him the satisfaction of knowing that. There would be no more snide, insulting remarks, no insinuations of blame—at least not from her and not for the next several days.

And after that? Well, he'd no longer be even remotely involved in her life and she would be free to forget him—if she could.

At the far end of the foyer, St. Julian's chief of police, immaculate in white Bermudas and short-sleeved white shirt, tucked his pith helmet under one arm and snapped to attention at their approach. "Inspector Montand at your service, *monsieur.* I am sorry to welcome you to our island under such unhappy circumstances."

Dominic nodded and came straight to the point. "Have you found my fiancée's body yet, Montand?"

If the inspector was offended by so blunt an approach, he didn't allow it to show. Ebony features impassive, he replied in the melodious island accent that Sophie found enchanting, "Sadly, we have not. The ocean currents beyond the reef, you understand, and the sharks..." His shrug, half Gallic, half native Caribbean, would have been comical at any other time. "We do not expect to find her, *monsieur.*"

"Her parents will find that very difficult to accept."

"I understand. *S'il vous plaît...*" He extended a pale palm in the direction of a trio of rattan chairs grouped beneath one of the many whirling ceiling fans. "Perhaps we could talk where it is cooler and more private?"

"How is it," Dominic asked when they were seated, "that no one thought to question my fiancée's ability to handle one of the hotel sailboats alone? It strikes me that the staff must bear some responsibility for her death."

Inspector Montand's gaze flickered beseechingly in Sophie's direction. She looked away and stared at an arrangement of tropical fruit on a side table, unwilling to help him out of what she knew to be a difficult spot.

The plain fact of the matter was that, practically from the moment she'd set foot on St. Julian, there had been any number of warnings leveled Barbara's way, and from more than one source, too.

It is not customary for unescorted ladies to behave so freely with employees, mademoiselle...

Barbara, you can't appear in public in that bikini! You'll offend the locals...

Mademoiselle, it is unwise to venture alone at night into the old section of town...

But Barbara had willfully ignored them all and instead seemed driven to excess in everything she'd done. She'd flirted outrageously with every male in sight; she'd partied with a frenzy that bordered on desperation. And, most recently, she'd taken to staying out all night, slinking back to the room she shared with Sophie just as the sun was rising. Her behavior had been downright embarrassing—not to mention downright odd for a woman supposedly in love and soon to be married.

Not that there hadn't been reason to question Barbara's devotion to her fiancé before then. "Dom's a wonderful catch," she'd boasted during one of her first conversations with Sophie. "Daddy says he's one of the few men who can afford me. Of course, he indulges my every whim, which is just as well because that's the sort of thing I've been used to all my life and I'm not about to settle for anything less just because I'm married."

Then she'd flashed her dazzling smile and shrugged as though to say she knew she sounded like a spoiled child but underneath she was really a charming, mature adult. As, indeed, she could be when it suited her. How else had she managed to wheedle Sophie into allowing her to tag along on the trip to the tiny island of St. Julian, a few hundred miles off the northeast coast of Venezuela?

Dominic's fingers rapping irritably on the glass-topped table brought Sophie back to the present with a start. "Well, Inspector, don't you agree? My fiancée didn't know one end of a boat from the other. As for raising a sail—the mere idea is absurd! She should never have been allowed—"

"As it happens, Monsieur Winter, Mademoiselle Wexler was not alone. According to hotel personnel who spoke with her on Wednesday morning and arranged for her to use the boat, she was accompanied by a member of the staff, a young man quite skilled at handling small craft such as the Laser."

"Then why the hell isn't he here now, answering my questions, instead of leaving you to do it?"

"Sad to say, he, too, was lost."

"Doesn't say much for his so-called skill, does it?" Dominic snapped.

The inspector shrugged apologetically. "The trouble appears to have been that they took the boat beyond the reef on the windward side of the island. Quite apart from the fact that a Laser is not meant to be sailed in the dangerous currents sweeping in from the Atlantic, it is also impossible for a person on shore to notice so small a vessel in distress. I am afraid that neither your fiancée nor the young man she hired as her crew showed very good sense when they chose to ignore the posted signs along that stretch of coast."

Dominic looked as if he might argue the point, then clamped his lips shut and glanced away. Sophie breathed a quiet sigh of relief. She would not have liked to be the one to corroborate what the chief inspector was trying so delicately to convey: that Barbara had invited her own disaster and was, perhaps, responsible for another person's death, too.

At length, Dominic turned back and this time leveled his bleak gaze on Sophie. "Where were you while all this was going on?"

"In the middle of town, photographing the water gardens outside the former governor's residence." Determined to let her better self prevail no matter how much he provoked her, she laid a sympathetic hand on his arm. "Mr. Winter—Dominic, I know it's hard not to want to lay blame on someone, but Barbara's death truly was an accident and the sooner you accept that, the sooner you'll begin to heal."

He shook her off as if she were an annoying little lapdog begging for favors. "It was an accident that could and should have been avoided. What was this employee thinking of that he sailed outside the reef to begin with?"

"I imagine because Barbara insisted he do so," Sophie said, exasperation winning out over tact and lending a decided edge to her voice. "She could be very persuasive when she wanted something, as I think we both know."

He dismissed the observation with an impatient shrug and turned back to Inspector Montand. "Have you called off the search?"

"*Oui, monsieur.* There is little point in continuing. The windward coast is extremely treacherous."

"I'll reserve judgment on that until I've seen the place for myself. This afternoon."

The police chief nodded deferentially. "I will arrange for you to be taken there."

"No need." Dominic cut him off with an autocratic wave of the hand and favored Sophie with another inimical glare. "You're reasonably familiar with the island, I take it?"

"Yes, I—"

"Then you can come with me."

Not "will you?" or "would you mind?" and certainly not a hint of a "please". Just another order, rapped out and expected to be obeyed without any regard for the fact that, for reasons that almost made her blush, she might not wish to be thrust into his company like this.

But he was not a mind reader, praise the Lord, so as much to put a speedy end to this whole sad business as to accommodate him, she stifled a refusal and said instead, "Of course."

"Where can we rent a car?" He ran a finger inside the collar of his open-necked shirt. "Preferably one equipped with air-conditioning."

"We can't—at least not the sort you have in mind."

"What? Why not?"

"Except for a very few registered government vehicles, there are no cars allowed on the island."

"You mean that open contraption decked out in flowers that brought me from the airport—"

"It's called a jitney. And it's one of only two on St. Julian."

An exasperated breath puffed from between his lips. "Then what's the alternative? Riding bareback on a donkey and waving a straw hat in the air?"

Chief Inspector Montand's posture, which would have done credit to the French Foreign Legion at the best of times, stiffened perceptibly. Sophie flung him a commiserating glance before saying mildly, "There's no need to be offensive, Mr. Winter. St. Julian might lack the sort of sophistication you're used to at home, but its other charms more than make up for that. We can take one of the mini-mokes provided by the hotel. It'll be more than adequate. The island is quite small."

Except for the streets in the center of town and the route from the airport, there was only one other paved road on St. Julian. The Coast Road, as its name suggested, ribboned around the perimeter of the island, dipping down at times into secluded coves and at others climbing to offer dizzying views of turquoise sea and jungle-clad mountains. Because its passage was so narrow, island custom dictated that traffic move always in a clockwise direction, even though that meant that a five mile trip out involved a twenty-five mile trip back again.

The little buggy, the fringe on its striped canvas canopy fluttering in the breeze, swooped merrily along with a scowling Dominic at the wheel. "I've driven more sophisticated golf carts," he grumbled as they jolted over one particularly vicious bump in the road.

"Would you prefer walking?" Sophie inquired, unable to disguise the sarcasm as they approached the next steep incline.

"I'd prefer not to be here at all," he shot back without a moment's hesitation. "Nor would I be, if it weren't for you and your half-baked ideas of a holiday paradise."

"St. Julian doesn't pretend to be Rio or Monte Carlo, Mr. Winter. If it did, I wouldn't bother wasting my time visiting it. The sort of people who flock to places like that don't particularly appeal to me."

The merest hint of a grin touched his lips. "People like me, you mean?"

She pulled off her sunglasses and subjected him to a frank examination, wondering if the extraordinary conditions of their mission might offer a glimpse past the good looks to the man within.

She was doomed to disappointment. Black hair swept back from a wide, intelligent brow. His nose had been broken at some point but had suffered not the least for the misfortune and merely enhanced the strong, uncompromising line of his profile. His eyes were the deep still green of woodland pools and his lashes would have been laughable had not the set of his jaw promised dreadful retribution to anyone who dared to make light of their beauty. As for the rest of him, it was so formidably and sexily masculine that he'd probably had to beat women off since the onset of puberty. But as far as giving a clue to his inner self? Not a one!

"What are you staring at?" he inquired testily, swiveling a glance at her.

"You," she replied. "I'm trying to figure out if you're this irascible all the time or if it's a temporary by-product of grief and heartache. I'm inclined to believe the latter since Barbara didn't strike me as the type who'd willingly devote the rest of her life to a chronic grouch."

He flung her another outraged glare before turning his attention once again to the road. "How much farther?" he barked.

"About seven miles. Once we round the headland, we drop down to the weather side of the island. You'll notice the change in the coastline immediately. It's very wild."

That he grew progressively more withdrawn as they covered the distance was indication enough that he agreed with her assessment. "Good God!" he muttered at one point, as spray flying across the windswept beach and on to the road caused visibility to shrink to a few yards. "Is it always like this?"

"More or less, though during the hurricane season it gets much worse."

"I'll take your word for it," he replied dryly. "Barbara must have been mad to consider trying to sail in this."

They were approaching the wind-battered southeastern tip of St. Julian, the place where Atlantic fury met the point of most resistance from the land mass. The shore there was littered with easy pickings for the beachcomber: driftwood forged into fantastic shapes, and seashells by the thousand in every shade from dark pearlescent purple to palest satin pink.

"There's a lookout point right ahead," Sophie said. "If you pull over, we can walk across the dunes and you'll see the reef where..."

He nodded, sparing her the necessity of having to elaborate, and swung the mini-moke off the road.

They clambered down to the beach and waded through the fine, soft sand. Then stood shoulder to shoulder and leaned into the wind, together yet separated by the intensely private silence in which Dominic wrapped himself.

A jagged line of surf marked the hidden reef. Close into shore the water swirled and foamed, subdued but by no means tamed by the barrier over which it had hurled itself. But beyond, where the heaving green Atlantic rollers let loose their fury... Dear Lord, Barbara must have been bent on suicide to have tried to sail in that, because no sane person could have hoped to survive such unleashed violence!

Sophie couldn't quell her shudder and looked away. Small wonder no trace of bodies had been found. It was a miracle the splintered wreckage of the Laser had endured the sort of beating it had taken.

Dominic, however, stared impassively for so long at the scene before him that Sophie half wondered if he'd forgotten her presence. Then, without warning, he swung toward her, his features stark with misery. "Get me the hell away from here before I really lose it," he muttered savagely.

He saw the dismay she couldn't hide, saw how it softened to compassion, and didn't know how he contained himself. He wanted to howl his outrage to the heavens; to curse and revile the cruelty and waste he'd been helpless to prevent. But the shock Sophie Casson now felt would be nothing compared to how she'd react if he really let loose his emotions. They boiled inside him with the same destructive fury of the seas out there, clenching his jaw, his fists, the ridged muscles of his abdomen.

"Dominic," she said, so softly he could barely hear her above the roar of the seas, "what can I do to help you?"

How certain she was that she understood him, how sure that she could assuage the misery. And how badly he wanted to smash her complacency! Out of the blue, a suggestion of the most outrageous magnitude sprang to mind, explicit, indecent.

Should he voice it? And would she accede to his wishes? Or would her wide gray eyes darken with horror as she backed away and began to run blindly as far from him as she could get?

He swiped at his hair with shaking fingers, appalled at the demons possessing him. Marshaling his features into a semblance of composure, he discarded the unconscionable and settled for the clichéd. "I think I would like to go back to the hotel and get thoroughly drunk. Would you care to join me?"

She was supposed to pucker up her sweet little mouth and simper that alcohol would merely add to his problems, not alleviate them. Instead, her eyes grew suspiciously bright and the next thing he knew, her tanned little hand with its short pink nails had tucked itself into the crook of his elbow. "Of course," she murmured sympathetically. "Anything you say."

And then she slipped her arm around his waist and led him back the way they'd come. Slowly, carefully, as if he were a very old, enfeebled man. The demons within itched to succumb to a black, unholy bellow of laughter. He could feel it pulsing deep in his chest and had one hell of a time suppressing it.

"Would you like me to drive?" she asked when they reached the toy that passed for transportation.

"No," he said, shrugging her off. Heaven forbid he should have a reason not to keep his eyes on the road!

Happy hour was well under way by the time they reached the hotel again. The sun hung just above the horizon, a great flaming ball far too large for its playground. Kerosene torches flickered palely among the trees in anticipation of the sudden rush of night typical of the tropics. Laughter and music combined to drown out the macaws' last screeching chorus of the day. It was party time. For everyone except Dominic Winter and Sophie Casson.

He decided it was in both their interests for him to ditch her and be alone to drown, if not his sorrows, then at least his guilt. "Look," he said, "I'm not fit company for a wolverine. What say we hold off on that drink until another time?"

She paused for as long as it took her to catch her lower lip between her teeth, then said, "Yes, of course. Actually, I'd just as soon go upstairs and take a shower before dinner." She rubbed at her bare arms and indicated the folds of her skirt. "The sea spray's—"

The last thing he needed was a guided tour on how the fabric clung damply to her long, slender thighs. "Whatever," he said rudely and, turning his back on her in a deliberate snub, headed straight for the bar and ordered a double brandy.

Let her think he was a sot. He didn't care, and the bottom line was he needed a little Dutch courage before he phoned the Wexlers. Not that anything he had to tell them would offer a grain of solace, but he'd promised he'd call and he would not willingly renege on a promise to them. If there was anything fine or good left within

him after all that had happened, it was his genuine
fondness for Barbara's parents.

Leaning both elbows on the bar, he stared down at
the drink in his hand. What a hell of a mess—a no-win
situation regardless of which way he looked at it! And
those paying the heaviest price were two people who deserved something better in their old age than the heart-
break of outliving their only child. He downed the
brandy in one gulp and raised a finger to the bartender
for a refill.

Dutch courage be damned! He wanted to be numbed
from the neck up. Maybe then he'd be able to banish
the demons possessing him.

CHAPTER TWO

BY THE time Sophie had bathed and changed, another flower-scented night had fallen, the third since Barbara's death. The cocktail crowd had gathered around the outdoor bar. She could hear their laughter mingling with the clink of ice on crystal and the throbbing beat of the steel drums. Was Dominic Winter part of that group, his brain sufficiently desensitized by alcohol that the edges of his pain had blurred? Or was he holed up in his room, determinedly drinking himself into oblivion?

"It's not your business, Sophie," she muttered, slipping silver and amethyst hoops on her ears. "Let him deal with what's happened on his own. It's safer that way."

Still, she found herself scanning the crowd, looking for him, when she went downstairs. He was not in the dining room, nor, as far as she could tell, was he outside on the wide, tiled patio. But the table she'd shared with no one since Wednesday tonight was again set for two.

She had finished the chilled cucumber soup and was halfway through her conch salad when he appeared. He wore the same open-necked white shirt and ecru linen trousers that he'd worn that afternoon. His hair had been combed repeatedly—by very irritable fingers. There was the faintest shadow of beard on his determined jaw. He looked like a man who'd had one too many—a man looking for trouble and ready to take on the entire world.

Forcibly reminding herself that he had just lost the woman he loved and was more to be pitied than reviled,

Sophie forbore to point out that adding a monumental hangover to his troubles would not make them any easier to bear. Instead, she nodded pleasantly and waited for him to make social overtures if, and when, he felt so inclined.

He quickly made it clear he did not feel inclined. "Looks like the hotel is determined to throw us together every chance they get," he remarked caustically, flinging himself into the seat opposite with rather more grace than one might have expected from a drunk. "Or did your Mother Teresa complex prompt you to request my company so that you could keep an eye on me in case despair drove me to the same sad end that Barbara suffered? Because if it did, I wish to hell you'd just butt out of my affairs."

His deft handling of the cutlery and lack of slurred speech gave Sophie pause. Dominic Winter was not drunk, as she had first supposed. He was a powder keg ready to explode—*wanting* to explode—and searching futilely for an excuse to do so. And there wasn't enough alcohol on St. Julian to do the job. He could have imbibed all night and still remained painfully sober. It was there for anyone to see in his smoldering green eyes. The torment was eating him alive.

"I'm not trying to interfere in your affairs," she said quietly. "I just want to do whatever I can to help."

He picked up the scrolled sheet of parchment on which the dinner menu had been printed and slid off the silk tassel encircling it. "It would help me enormously if you'd get on with your meal without feeling the need to engage me in conversation. And it would help me even more if you'd do so quickly and then quietly disappear."

Normally, Sophie would have refused on principle to do any such thing, even given that his painstaking rudeness had robbed her of her appetite. But in his present mood, she had no more wish to spend time with him than he had with her. So why did she half rise from her seat, then pause uncertainly as if about to change her mind, thereby giving him opportunity to insult her further?

Sensing her hesitation, he glared out from behind the parchment. "I do not want your company, Ms. Casson, nor do I need it," he declared brusquely.

Cheeks flaming, she dropped her napkin beside her plate and, like the spineless ninny she undoubtedly must be, scuttled away.

She did not see him again until the following evening. "*Monsieur* has gone to police headquarters with Chief Inspector Montand, to take care of the necessary paperwork, you understand," the clerk at the front desk told her when she stopped by shortly after breakfast the next morning. "Such a shocking loss of a life can never be dismissed lightly, *mademoiselle*." He wrinkled his nose as though to imply that only someone as inconsiderate as Barbara would behave so boorishly in alien territory. "*Hélas*, that is especially true in the case of foreigners who die while they are here."

Sophie understood. Fellow guests who'd been friendly enough before the tragedy avoided her now as though afraid she'd somehow cast an evil spell on her friend and might do the same to them. If there'd been any way to cut her holiday short she'd have done so on the spot, but there were only two flights a week in and out of St. Julian, on Tuesdays and Fridays. Whether she liked it or not, she was prisoner there for another four days.

She spent the afternoon at an orchid farm and returned late to the hotel, leaving herself with barely enough time to shower and change for the evening meal.

To her surprise, Dominic was already seated at the table when she went down to the dining room.

"Ah, Ms. Casson," he murmured, rising smoothly and pulling out her chair, "I was hoping you'd favor me with your presence again tonight."

He looked quite devastating in pale gray trousers and shirt. Urbane, sophisticated and thoroughly in control of himself and the situation.

Very much on her guard, Sophie said, "Were you? Well, I hate to add to your troubles, Mr. Winter, but if you're hoping to drive me off again by plying me with insults, I'm afraid you're in for a disappointment. I'm far too hungry to allow you to get away with it a second time."

Even after only one day of tropical sun, his olive skin was burnished with color, so it was difficult to be sure but she thought perhaps he blushed a little at that, an assumption that gained credence with his next words. "I'm afraid I behaved very badly last night," he said contritely. "I must beg your pardon. I wasn't at my best."

You don't have a best! she felt like informing him. Except she didn't really believe that. She'd thought for a long time that he was far too good for Barbara. She'd even gone so far as to wish....

Conscience-stricken, she picked up the menu and pretended to read it. Bad enough she'd allowed herself to fantasize when Barbara was alive. To do so now was tantamount to dancing on her grave!

Glancing up, Sophie found his gaze trained on her face. He was different tonight. The rage in his eyes had been replaced by a clouded emptiness as though the reality of Barbara's death had at last sunk in and he realized no amount of ranting or blaming was going to bring her back.

Sophie almost preferred the other Dominic, the one breathing fire and condemnation. That one moved her to anger despite her better nature; this one moved her to pity—dangerous territory at the best of times.

"I really do apologize," he said.

"Apology accepted." She shrugged and searched for another subject, one that would draw her attention away from his broad shoulders and the burden they carried. He was a Samson of a man not intended to be broken, but Barbara's death had brought him perilously close to the edge. "What looks good for dinner, do you think?"

After some discussion, he ordered turtle steak and she the fish caught fresh that morning. "And wine," he decided, adding with a faint inflection of humor, "Don't worry, I'll behave. I'm a man of fairly temperate habits and don't, as a rule, choose to drown my sorrows in drink."

He was trying to be charming and succeeding, and she wished he'd stop. It made too great an assault on her defenses, leaving her vulnerable to the most preposterous urge to comfort him. It was a relief when their food arrived. It gave her something else to do with hands that ached to reach out and touch his long, restless fingers; to cup his cheek and stroke the severe line of his mouth. To pillow his head against her breast...

He'd probably deck her! He wanted glamorous Barbara Wexler, not unremarkable Sophie Casson, and would almost certainly view any attempt on the latter's part to share his grief as unforgivably presumptuous.

"What did you do today?" he asked, interrupting her line of thought and, when she told him, said, "Do you get many ideas from your travels abroad? For your work, I mean?''

He was no more interested in her answer than was she in his question, but meaningless small talk was safer than silence that allowed her mind to stray to thoughts better left unexplored.

''I remember the first time we met,'' he remarked later, staring absently into his glass of wine. ''You were halfway up a tree on the Wexler estate, wearing dungarees covered in mud and with a camera slung around your neck.''

''And you thought I was trespassing. You were ready to throw me off the property.''

He nodded. ''Yes. I knew they'd hired a landscape architect to design a waterfall and lily pond, but you hardly fitted the description. I'd expected—''

''What?'' she snapped, welcoming the surge of annoyance his words inspired. ''A man?''

''Not necessarily. Just someone more . . . professional-looking.''

''Tell me, Mr. Winter,'' Sophie shot back, ''when you first started out in the construction business, did you show up on the job wearing a three-piece suit?''

He smiled, such a rare and pleasant change from his usual gravity. ''As a matter of fact, I did. I'd decided to buy five adjacent properties, all very run-down, and wanted to impress my bank manager into lending me the money to complete the sale. And I think we should drop the Mr. Winter–Ms. Casson thing. It seems to breed hostility between us and we've got enough to deal with, without that.''

''If there's hostility,'' Sophie couldn't help retorting, ''it's of your making, not mine, and has been ever since we met.''

She expected he'd argue the point but he didn't. He merely raised his elegant black brows and shrugged. "I daresay you're right," he admitted. "But that was then and this is now. Things have changed."

His habitually somber expression was firmly back in place. It was hard to imagine him succumbing to flighty Barbara's charms; harder still to picture him lowering his icy reserves and making love to her.

The audacity of such speculation sent a wash of color over Sophie's cheeks. "Um..." she said, nearly choking on a morsel of fish, "I wonder if the Wexlers will still want me about the place after this. Have you spoken with them since...?"

His manner became even more guarded than usual. "I called them last night."

"They must be—"

"They're devastated."

Sophie sighed, thinking of the gentle elderly couple whose entire existence had revolved around the daughter who'd arrived on the scene so late in their lives. "Yes," she said softly. "To outlive your children is completely contrary to the proper order of nature. I can only imagine how difficult they must be finding it."

"Try 'impossible'," he suggested shortly. "Nothing you imagine can begin to equate with what they're going through. At this point, I doubt they're fully able to comprehend it themselves." The animosity that, fleetingly, had faded from his eyes, resurfaced. "And I'm quite sure they won't want you around to remind them of what they've lost. At the very least, stay away until you hear from them—or better yet, from me. In fact, it might be best for everyone if you were to delegate someone else from your company to complete your share of the landscape project."

Sophie stared at him over the rim of her glass. "It really doesn't come as much of a surprise that you'd assume I'm too lacking in tact or respect to show any sensitivity toward the Wexlers, so I won't waste my breath trying to counteract your opinion," she said, nothing in her demeanor betraying the hurt his remark had inflicted. "I can live with the fact that you don't much like me, Mr. Winter, but I will not tolerate your repeated insinuations that Barbara's death was in any way my fault, and I will not allow you to drive me into hiding. If and when the Wexlers are ready to have me finish the job *they* hired me to do, I shall make myself available."

"It would be better for all of us if you stayed away," he maintained obstinately, and for all that she tried to stem it, another blast of hurt shafted through her at the unbending accusation in his voice. She could protest until the world stopped turning but, just as it was clear nothing could alter his initial antipathy toward her, so it was equally clear that he still held her accountable for the pain he was now suffering.

She was sorely tempted to get up and leave, but pride wouldn't let her be put to rout two nights in a row. So, willing her voice not to betray her by trembling, she said, "In that case, why don't you ask to sit somewhere else for the duration of your stay here? Because heaven forbid I should cause you indigestion on top of all my other manifest sins."

Sophie didn't know whether or not he'd taken her suggestion to heart because she walked into town for breakfast on Sunday, spent the rest of the morning in the botanical gardens and stopped at a roadside stand for a lunch consisting of a sandwich and freshly squeezed fruit juice cocktail.

It was after two when she got back to the hotel and the breeze that normally made the heat tolerable had died completely. Out of respect for Barbara, she'd abandoned her habit of skin diving in the lagoon beyond the palm-fringed beach each afternoon, and spent the time instead with a book under an umbrella on the patio. But that day, fatigued as much by the fact that she hadn't slept well the night before as by the hot Caribbean sun, she slipped into a bikini and stretched out on a wicker chaise in the restful shade of her balcony. That she was also going out of her way to avoid Dominic Winter and his cold, disapproving gaze was something she preferred not to acknowledge.

The murmur of the ocean, in concert with the musical splash of the fountains in the gardens below, soothed like a lullaby. All the hard-edged events of the past few days softened, their colors paling to dreamy pastels. Lassitude spread through Sophie's arms, her legs, and she welcomed it, happy to drift in the no-man's-land between waking and sleeping.

She didn't notice when the colors faded to black or the languor took complete possession of her mind as well as her body. She knew nothing until she became suddenly and alarmingly conscious of someone moving about in her room.

There were discreet signs posted throughout the hotel, warning guests to keep their bedroom doors locked and all valuables stored in the safe at the front desk. Sophie had no valuables worth worrying about except for her camera equipment, and she was reasonably certain she'd locked her door, but there was no doubt someone had managed to gain access. Slewing her gaze sideways, she could see through the slats of the louvered balcony doors the shadow of a man moving back and forth within the room.

A glance at her watch showed that more than an hour had passed since she'd apparently fallen asleep. Time enough for a seasoned burglar to pick the lock and go about his business. His mistake, however, lay in choosing a victim who'd already been on the receiving end of Dominic Winter's unabashed displeasure. She was in no mood to take further abuse from anyone else.

Without stopping to consider the wisdom of such a move, she slid off the chaise and moved swiftly around the half-open door. But the outrage she'd been about to vent at the intruder dwindled to wordless shock at the sight before her.

Dominic was naked from the waist up, his torso in all its sleekly muscled beauty narrowing to fit snugly into the waist of khaki linen shorts. And yet, that was not quite accurate. Although invisible, desolation hung about him like a second presence.

He stood before the low dresser that still contained Barbara's things, his broad shoulders paralleling the bowed despair of his dark head. In the palm of his hand lay the diamond ring he'd given her, even its bright fire temporarily dimmed.

Sophie's breath escaped in a soft exhalation of protest at being too long trapped in her throat. The sound looped across the mourning hush that filled the room and wound itself around him, bringing his head up and swinging around to face her. His eyes were the deep dark green of moss clothing ancient gravestones. And his mouth...!

Her heart contracted with pity, leaving no room for the anger and hurt she'd nurtured from the night before. "Dominic," she breathed, and cupped her hands in front of her as if they held the magic formula guaranteed to wipe away his hurt.

He blinked and focused his gaze on her slowly, the way a person does when emerging from deep sleep. "They told me you were gone for the day," he said, his voice a husky echo of its usual rich baritone. "I thought it would be a good time to take care of...this."

His fingers closed around the ring, his other hand gesturing at the contents of the open drawer. Little bits of silk and ribbon-trimmed lingerie frothed in disorder, just the way Barbara had left them. Her suitcase lay open on Sophie's bed, one half already filled with items from her share of the closet.

Still poised near the balcony doors, Sophie nodded understanding. "I would have done it myself, except I didn't feel it was my place."

"It wasn't your responsibility." Impatiently, Dominic tossed the ring on top of the articles of clothing remaining in the drawer and, scooping everything up in both hands, turned to stuff it in the suitcase.

As he did so, something slid out from between the folds of fabric and slipped to the floor despite Sophie's attempt to catch it. It was the tooled-leather picture frame that, for the first few days of the holiday, had sat on the bedside table next to Barbara's bed. Hinged in the middle, it contained two photographs, one of Dominic and one of Barbara.

Stooping, Sophie retrieved it and passed it to him. He sank to the edge of Barbara's bed and for the longest time stared at the image of his dead fiancée.

Not a trace of emotion showed on his face. The seconds slowed, tightening the already-tense atmosphere so painfully that Sophie wished she'd ignored her scruples and simply taken charge of packing Barbara's things herself.

At last, Dominic slapped the frame closed the way a man does a book that, regretfully, he's finished reading for all that he never wanted it to end. But instead of completing packing Barbara's things, he remained where he was, hands idle, with the photograph frame clasped between them.

Yet another goodbye, Sophie thought, sympathy welling within her. *He must wonder if they'll ever end.*

Covering the small distance that separated them, she perched next to him and gently removed the frame from his hands. Unwillingly, he looked at her, the expression in his eyes veiled by the thick fringe of his lashes.

He did not want her to see his grieving, as though there was something shameful in allowing himself to succumb to it. She knew because her brother, Paul, was just the same.

What was it about men that what they accepted as healthy and normal in a woman they saw as weakness in themselves? Didn't they know the healing took longer if it was denied? That only by accepting it and dealing with it could they validate eventual recovery from it?

Seeing Dominic closing in on himself and refusing to let go, Sophie could only suppose they didn't, and so she offered comfort exactly as she'd have extended it to anyone, man, woman or child, in the same state of grief. With one hand she reached up and brought his head down to her shoulder, and with the other raised his fingertips to her mouth and kissed them.

For an instant, he resisted. She felt his opposition in the sudden rigidity of his arm, heard it in the hissing intake of his breath. And then, like a house of cards caught in a sudden draft of air, he collapsed against her, the weight of him catching her off guard and pushing her backward on the bed. He followed, his face buried at her neck, his hands tangling in her hair, his legs entwined with hers.

He smelled of soap and clear blue skies and sun-drenched ocean, all bound together by lemon blossoms. His skin, more bronzed than ever, scalded where it touched, the heat of him a strange elixir that penetrated her pores to coil within her bloodstream.

At least, she thought it did—as much as she was capable of thought. Because what had begun as a reaching out in commiseration changed course dramatically, though exactly how and when escaped her. One minute she and Dominic were behaving with the decorum of two people sitting side by side in church, and the next they were rolling around on the brightly patterned bedspread with the hungry abandon of lovers.

Somehow, his mouth found hers and fastened to it, seeking comfort wherever it was to be found. How could she have known the shape it would take, how have avoided what happened next?

Without volition, her lips opened. She felt the heat of his breath, the moisture of his tongue accepting the invitation so flagrantly offered. There was no use pretending it was an accidental and utterly chaste collision of two mouths intent on other things, because it was not. It was a wrong and unprincipled and utterly, irresistibly erotic prelude to even greater sin.

Without warning, the cool and distant Dominic Winter she'd known metamorphosed into a lover as swiftly as night fell on St. Julian.

Of course, *he* could be excused. He was not himself. He was ripped apart with anguish, lost, lonely...oh, there was any number of reasons for *him* to behave irrationally. But what was her justification? Why did she wind her arms around his neck as if she never wanted to let him go, then kiss him back and let him touch her near naked body in its pitifully brief little bikini that she'd never have countenanced wearing in public?

Why, when he pushed aside the spaghetti straps holding up the bra, did she shift to accommodate him? And when he stroked her breasts, then lowered his head to kiss them, why did she arch toward him with about as much restraint as a drowning woman reaching for a lifeline? How could she explain the rush of damp heat between her thighs or the aching drumroll of desire building within her womb?

She knew why. This wasn't some sudden tropical fever robbing her of propriety or decency; it was a slow-growing affliction that had begun months ago. That day in the Wexlers' garden, it had been the impact of his cool green inspection, and not her rapid descent from the tree, that had sent her practically sprawling at his feet. He'd stood there like some beautiful avenging angel, and despite the disapproval manifest in his gaze and in his voice, something inside her had responded to him in a very primal way. He'd ignited a spark that had been waiting for a chance to burst into flame.

She'd tried to ignore it, heaven knew. It had been the only sane course to follow, given that, in addition to his overt disaffection for her, he was also engaged to marry Barbara. A woman would have to be blind as well as stupid to think for a moment that a man—*any* man— would look twice at ordinary Sophie Casson if fascinating Barbara Wexler was his for the taking.

But that was then and this was now. Barbara had gone, and for whatever reason, Dominic had turned to her, Sophie. Even in the midst of passion, she knew he was trying to lose himself, to forget, if only for a little while, his pain. And if it was shameful to welcome the chance to assuage his need, then she was guilty. Because wild dogs would not have deterred her at that moment.

He stripped away her bikini bottom, fumbled with the belt at his waist, and she helped him, her fingers nimble at the buttoned fly of his khaki shorts. He rolled to one side, shrugged himself free of the confinement of clothing, and then he was covering her again. Covering her, and entering her, hot, frenzied, reckless.

She took him into herself. Absorbed his pain, his loss, and made it hers. Did whatever she had to do, gave everything he silently begged of her, to make things more bearable for him. If it had been within her power, she'd have brought Barbara back, even though doing so would have made her own loneliness more acute.

And why? Never mind why. The reason wasn't to be entertained. To allow it even momentary lodging in her mind would be to invite misery into her heart as a permanent guest. Instead, she shut out her own needs and catered to his.

He drove himself as if the hounds of hell were in pursuit and he was desperate to outrace them. Willingly, Sophie raced with him, her peripheral awareness shrinking as a great roaring flood gathered inside her. There was not a force in this world or any other that could have stopped either of them.

And then it was over as suddenly as it had begun and there was nothing but the sound of sudden rain splashing on the tropical shrubs outside and dimpling the surface of the pool. As if the sun couldn't bear to witness such wanton conduct and had ordered the rain to wash away the shame of it all.

Looking anywhere but at her, Dominic rolled into a sitting position, reached for his clothes and climbed into them even more speedily than he'd shed them. She thought he'd simply walk out of the room and that would be that, but he didn't. Instead, he stood at the open balcony doors and stared out.

Unable to bear his silence a moment longer, Sophie slid to her feet, wrapping herself in the flowered bedspread as she did so, and went to stand beside him. "Say something, Dominic," she begged.

His shoulders rose in a great sigh. An unguarded sorrow formed in the curve of his mouth, then in his eyes as they focused on the distance beyond the windows. As if he was watching a ship bearing a loved one disappear over the horizon. "What in God's name can I say?"

A slow trembling began inside her, gathering force as it spread until she shook from head to foot. She was the one who'd started everything when she'd reached out and touched him. It was all her fault.

"Tell me that you don't hate me for what I allowed to happen," she whispered. "That you don't think it was something I planned. I feel guilty enough without that."

He swung his head toward her and she thought she had never looked into such emptiness as she found in his eyes. When he spoke, his voice was raw with...what? Rage, pain, regret?

"Right now," he said, "I don't give a rat's rear how you're feeling. I'm too busy despising myself."

Once again, he reduced her to such shock that her knees almost buckled beneath her as the blood rushed from her face. But he didn't notice, nor would he probably have cared. Snatching up Barbara's suitcase, he rammed it shut. Then he stalked across the room to the door, opened it, stepped through and closed it quietly behind him. And just to add salt to Sophie's wounds, the rain passed as suddenly as it had begun and the sun came out again.

She did not go down for dinner that night. She took a long, too-hot bath and tried to scrub away the shame and the hurt. And then, while people laughed and danced on the patio below, she lay in her bed and tried to ignore its twin standing empty only a few feet away.

But even though the night was moonless, the hurricane lamps in the garden flung up enough of a glow for her to see the other bed's outline quite clearly. Its pillows sat not quite straight and one corner of the flowered cover trailed on the floor. As though whoever had thrown it back in place had done so carelessly. Or furtively, because its disarray had been caused by people who had no business lying on it in the first place, let alone making unseemly imitation love there.

Shame flowed over Sophie again, more invasive even than Dominic's hands, licking over every inch of her skin, into every secret curve and fold until she burned from its onslaught. How *could* she have allowed herself?

If only Elaine hadn't fallen victim to the chicken pox. If only she hadn't agreed to let Barbara take Elaine's place! Why had she when, of all people, Barbara Wexler was a woman with whom she shared nothing in common?

She knew why. For the sadistic pleasure of listening to Barbara talk about her fiancé. For vicarious thrills. Because, from the outset, Sophie had wanted him.

Well, now she'd had him, however briefly. And she felt like the lowest form of life ever to slither across the face of the earth.

CHAPTER THREE

IN THE hours following, Sophie learned that it didn't take sleep for a person to find herself trapped in a nightmare. Much though she would have liked to divert them, disturbing questions raced through her mind. Had he known to whom he'd just made such desperate love? Was it Sophie Casson with her conscience, like her mind, clouded by a raging hunger, who'd filled him with passion—or Barbara's ghost taking up temporary residence for one last farewell?

Worn out with anguish, Sophie fell asleep just before dawn and awoke a short time later to a day luminous with sun and that special clarity of light indigenous to the Caribbean. Her immediate reaction was to bury her head under the pillows and remain there well into the next century, but a thump on her door put an end to such wishful thinking.

Probably the maid, she thought drearily. But it was Dominic, the very last person in the world she wanted to face with her hair standing on end and her eyes red ringed from hours of on-again, off-again crying.

He stared at her, the turmoil he was suffering plain to see. From the beginning of their association, he'd struck her as a man of many layers, all of them designed to keep her at a distance. He wore pride over arrogance, distaste over reserve, hauteur over grief, drawing each one around himself like a cloak. And now, on top of them all, his raging disgust for having allowed her to glimpse that vulnerable side of himself that she suspected he seldom acknowledged even to himself.

Without invitation, he stepped into the room and shouldered the door closed. Too dismayed to ask what he thought he was doing barging in on her like that, she backed away from him, cringing inwardly at the bars of sunlight slanting through the louvered windows to reveal her in all her disheveled glory.

"I expected you'd be awake already," he said, following her.

She tugged furtively on the hem of her nightshirt, which came only midway down her thighs. "I am—now."

His beautiful brows shot upward as though he thought only the most dissolute of creatures would still be in bed at such an hour, but at least he had the good grace not to voice the opinion aloud. "I just came back from a meeting with Inspector Montand. All the red tape's taken care of finally, so I'm free to leave. I'll be on my way within a couple of hours."

That's all he knew! "There isn't another flight out until tomorrow afternoon," Sophie informed him, a certain malicious satisfaction at being one step ahead of him for a change coloring her tone.

His gaze slewed past her as if he found the sight of her singularly offensive. "For other people, perhaps, but I'm not prepared to wait that long, so I've chartered a private jet. If you care to, you're welcome to come with me. I can't imagine you're still in a holiday mood after everything that's happened."

He was right. More than anything, she wanted to escape from this island and all its painful memories. But the thought of spending ten or more hours in the undiluted company of a man who clearly viewed her with a combination of embarrassment and disgust was even less appealing. "Thanks anyway, but I think I should stick to my original travel plans."

His gaze flickered to Barbara's bed and away again. "Yes," he conceded. "Perhaps that would be best."

His attitude, and the way he abruptly turned and left, reminded her of another time earlier that fall. Sophie had started work at the Wexlers' about nine on a morning so damp and dreary that Mrs. Wexler had insisted she come in out of the cold and have lunch with them.

She hadn't found it a particularly relaxed meal. The Wexlers were kind and called her "Sophie" and "dear". Barbara, who seemed compelled to abbreviate everyone's name but her own, called her "Sophe". But Dominic had steadfastly stuck to "Ms. Casson"—on those few occasions that he called her anything at all.

"So you're still here, Ms. Casson," he'd said when he came upon her still hard at it later that afternoon. "Does that mean you'll be joining us for dinner, too?"

From his tone, one would have thought she made a habit of cadging free meals! "No," she'd assured him, aware as always of the undeclared currents of war flowing between them. "I'm an employee, not a friend of the family, and hardly belong at the dinner table."

"It might be a good idea for us all to remember that," he'd replied enigmatically, then stalked away, just as he did now, without bothering to say goodbye. An adversarial, uncivil man, she'd decided at the time, his exquisitely tailored suits and elegant black Jaguar with its pale gray leather upholstery notwithstanding.

Well, the war had been waged at last, and Barbara's bed had been the battlefield. The question was, had anyone emerged a winner?

She didn't see him again. By the time she came downstairs he'd already left, and her last day on St. Julian
was uneventful. The next afternoon, she left, too, and
slept that night in her own bed, comforted by the knowledge that once she'd sent flowers and a note of con-
dolence to the Wexlers, it would be over, all of it.

But it wasn't. The following week, she got a call from
Barbara's mother. "I wonder, my dear, if you'd come
to see us and tell us, if you will, what you know...?"
Gail Wexler's voice broke, and a stifled sob punctuated
the brief silence before she was able to continue. "Please,
will you come, Sophie? You were the last person to see
our daughter alive, and if we could talk to you, it might
help us to...accept what's happened."

It required a colder heart than Sophie possessed to
refuse. Nothing would be over for any of them, she
realized then, until all the rituals of grieving had been
observed. "When would you like to see me?"

They settled on the following evening at eight o'clock.
When Sophie pulled up in her car, she found Dominic's
Jaguar already parked in the driveway outside the house.
She'd half expected he'd be in attendance, too, since the
Wexlers clearly regarded him as a son, and she had
thought herself prepared to cope with the eventuality.
Still, when he opened the mansion's front door to her,
the sight of his unsmiling face unsettled her badly.

I let him make love to me, she thought, appalled all
over again. *I shared the ultimate intimacy with a man
whom I knew to be in love with someone else at the
time.*

Something of her dismay must have showed on her
face because as soon as she'd greeted the Wexlers in the
drawing room, Dominic took her by the elbow and

steered her to a side table where a silver coffee service waited.

Under the pretext of filling a cup for her, he said in a low tone, "Please try to hide your aversion to being here. It isn't pleasant for any of us, but you don't have to make it any harder on the Wexlers than it already is."

"I'm fully aware of that," she said softly, annoyance at his choosing once again to interpret her actions in the most unfavorable light diminished by her shock at the change in Barbara's parents. They had aged dreadfully over the past few weeks and seemed terribly fragile.

But Dominic wasn't done harassing her. "Furthermore," he decreed in that bossy way of his, "although I gathered from Montand that you pretty well agreed with him when he intimated that Barbara asked for trouble down on St. Julian, her parents don't need to be told that."

It was the verbal slap in the face needed to restore Sophie. "I wouldn't dream of it," she muttered indignantly. "What sort of person do you take me for?"

"You don't want to know," he shot back, lowering his lashes to hide the scorn flaring in his eyes.

Mrs. Wexler patted the cushion beside her on the brocade sofa. "Bring your cup and sit here with me, Sophie. We're so grateful to you for coming tonight and I know we'll both feel better for your visit. Won't we, John?"

If anything, Barbara's father looked even frailer than his wife. "She was only twenty-four," he murmured plaintively. "I don't understand how someone so young and full of life could be snuffed out like that. Why did it happen?"

"I think perhaps because she *was* so full of life, just as you say, Mr. Wexler," Sophie suggested, trying hard to tread the fine path between honesty and tact. "She was impatient..."

Apparently, she hadn't tried hard enough. From his post at the corner of the fireplace, Dominic frowned a caution. "'Eager' might be a better word, Ms. Casson."

So might "rebellious", Sophie thought, *not to mention "selfish" and "willful" and "downright cheap"*. But of course, he didn't want to hear that sort of thing, any more than the Wexlers did, and who was she to belittle anyone else's morals in light of her own fall from grace?

"But was she having fun...until...?"

The pathetic hope in Mrs Wexler's next question broke Sophie's heart. It was a relief to be able to say quite truthfully that, until the accident, Barbara had been busy having a wonderful time on St. Julian. Fortunately, neither parent asked Sophie to elaborate on the remark.

"There'll be a service next week in the Palmerstown Memorial Chapel, and a plaque placed in the gardens," Dominic informed her when he saw her out. "The Wexlers would appreciate your being there."

"Of course." Resigned, Sophie nodded. Just this one last observance out of respect to the Wexlers and then it truly would be over, all of it. She could go back to her own life, her own friends, and there'd be nothing to remind her of the senseless tragedy that had taken place on a tiny island just off the coast of South America.

Nothing, that was, except for the lingering memory of Dominic Winter's kiss, the inexcusable longing to feel his touch again—and, as the following days turned into weeks and two months slid quietly by, the horrifying suspicion that the past was not going to fade quietly away after all.

By the time February howled in on a blizzard, she was terribly afraid that she was to be left with the most permanent reminder possible, in the shape of Dominic's child.

What with Christmas and the painful emptiness it brought to the Wexlers, then the chore of organizing the mess of paperwork on his desk that always accumulated at the end of the fiscal year, Dominic found it easy enough to put off what he knew, sooner or later, had to be done. Not that he wouldn't have preferred to act as if nothing had happened. Hell, he'd spent most of his waking hours since regretting the single moment of weakness that had undermined everything he prided himself on possessing: integrity, decency, loyalty, fidelity.

Of course, there were some who'd say he deserved to be cut down to size. He'd stepped on more than a few toes in his drive to reach the top and been called a lot of unflattering things on the way. "Cutthroat" and "ruthless" didn't begin to do justice to some of the adjectives that had been applied to Dominic Winter, the man who'd built a fortune on hard work and a willingness to take chances, and who now owned half the real estate in Palmerstown as proof that the gamble had paid off.

But other people's opinions had never struck him as worth losing sleep over as long as his own sense of self-respect remained intact. He supported worthy causes, donated his share and then some to make sure that mothers, children and old people didn't wind up homeless on the streets of Palmerstown. Neither did he play fast and loose with married women or investors' money.

He paid an honest day's wage for an honest day's work, no employee of Winter Development Corporation ever had to worry that ill health would cost him his job, and every person on his payroll found a fat bonus included in his December paycheck. Given all that, looking in the mirror every morning and seeing an unprincipled schmuck of thirty-five staring back at him was a bit more than Dominic could stomach.

He didn't bother to phone her ahead of time. She'd probably hang up on him or else suggest he take his belated concern and perform some anatomically impossible act with it. Instead, late on the eighth Sunday after Barbara's memorial service, he looked up Sophie Casson's address and drove to the outskirts of town where she lived to pay her a surprise visit. Why go about it any differently? It seemed to be the story of their whole association after all, her tripping over him when she least expected it. No point in breaking the mold now.

It was another bitter night, but at least the snow had stopped and a ragged moon shed enough light for him to see the lopsided little house where she lived and, beyond it, the wind-ruffled surface of Jewel Lake. A well-situated piece of property, he surmised, and one which, at any other time, he'd have been itching to see put to more attractive use. But he wasn't ringing her doorbell as a developer; he was coming, metaphorical hat in hand, to make overdue apology for taking sexual advantage of her and to make sure there weren't any unwelcome surprises lurking on the horizon as a result of his rash behavior.

It took her a moment or two to answer. He heard her footsteps as she ran down the stairs, saw her shadow loom closer through the frosted-glass panes on either side of the entrance, and then the front door opened and light spilled out into the night to show her the face of her visitor.

To say she was surprised to see him was an understatement. In fact, he was across the threshold before it seemed to register with her that her eyes were not deceiving her.

Her reaction then was out of all proportion to the situation and scarcely flattering. She'd obviously not been home long herself. She wore high-topped leather boots, and had left her coat slung over the newel at the foot of the stairs. From the small empty bag stamped with the name of the local drugstore, which she held in one hand, it would appear she'd been shopping.

When she realized that he was not simply an unpleasant figment of her imagination, she clutched the bag to her as if it contained the crown jewels of England and stared at him, her gray eyes huge in the sudden pallor of her face. "Have you been following me?" she demanded, her voice unnaturally shrill.

He stared at her, genuinely perplexed. "Why the hell would I be doing that?"

She opened her mouth to tell him, then seemed to think better of the idea and clamped it shut again.

"Look, Ms. Casson . . ." he began forcefully, until the absurdity of calling her Ms. after the intimacy they'd shared stopped him dead. He raked a hand through his hair and started again. "Sophie, please! I'm here because I'm concerned."

"Concerned?" she repeated in that same high, brittle voice. "Concerned about what? I'm perfectly all right. Why on earth wouldn't I be?"

This was not the same woman who'd dealt so calmly with events on St. Julian. This was a woman on the verge of falling apart and he wasn't sure he wanted to know why. "No reason," he said offhandedly. "I just wanted to make sure, that's all. If nothing else, I feel I owe you an apology, even if I can't offer an explanation for what happened down in the Caribbean."

"Nothing happened," she said, her face flushing. "You don't owe me anything."

He sighed, a strange disappointment overtaking him. "I suppose it's too much to expect that we might just once sit down and talk like normal, civilized people?"

At that, it seemed to occur to her that her behavior was not entirely rational and she made an effort to gather herself together a bit. "No, of course not." She gestured toward an open doorway. "There's a fire set in the living room, if you'd like to go in. I'll join you as soon as I've hung up my coat."

It was a tiny, late 1920s house, he'd guess, and not particularly well built by today's standards. The fire she'd mentioned had not been started, leaving the room at the mercy of drafts creeping in through the cracks around the windows.

Squatting down before the grate, he piled a little more kindling atop the pyramid she'd built, then felt inside the chimney to make sure the damper was open. He was rewarded with a shower of soot speckling his hand and the cuff of his shirt.

"Oh dear!" she exclaimed from the doorway. "I should have warned you not to touch that. It sticks."

"So I gather," he said dryly. "How do you ever manage to get a decent fire going?"

She grimaced, pursing her lips and wrinkling her nose in a way that he found rather charming. "Actually, I seldom do."

"Small wonder. Will it offend your notions of feminine emancipation if I offer to fix it for you?" He surveyed his filthy hands ruefully. "I'd hate to think I ended up looking like a chimney sweep for nothing."

Her smile more than made up for the antagonism she'd shown earlier. "I'd be very grateful. On really cold days

I have to bring in an electric heater to make the room bearable.''

"Do you rent this place? Because if you do, it's your landlord's—"

"I own it," she said. "If you discount the rather hefty mortgage, that is."

"Ever think of selling?" He wrenched hard on the lever that controlled the damper and received another liberal dousing of soot.

"No. The house might not amount to much, but the garden…!" She sighed and hugged her arms. "It's lovely and more than makes up for any other shortcomings."

"I should have expected an answer like that. I remember how you drooled over the Wexlers' arboretum."

Bad move! he realized at once. By alluding to the Wexlers, he'd brought back reminders of a time he and Sophie both preferred to forget. Her expression, which moments before had become more open and relaxed, closed like a limpet.

"Well," he said hastily, ramming the damper lever more securely into a niche inside the brick-lined chimney, "that's about the best I can do for now, but if you like, I'll send over one of my workers to fix it permanently. Is there some place I can clean up a bit?"

"The bathroom's at the top of the stairs," she told him. "First door on the right."

She left him to find his own way and disappeared into the kitchen.

Before he reached the upper landing, he heard the whir of some small kitchen appliance, followed almost immediately by the aroma of freshly ground coffee.

At the top of the stairs, a small brass lamp set on an old military trunk illuminated the photograph of a mustachioed man in uniform standing next to it. A swag of dried flowers tied with a cream silk ribbon hung above a small oriel window. Cosy little touches that played no part in the austere decor of Dominic's penthouse, and which he'd never missed until now, when, somewhat to his surprise, he found himself envying the leggy blonde in the kitchen downstairs.

She might not enjoy the sort of luxury with which he'd surrounded himself, but she'd found something else, something rarer: a sense of home, of belonging, that he'd never known. It showed in the ambience she'd created in her funny little house. It showed in her smile when she allowed it to emerge, and in her eyes when she talked about her garden and the work she loved.

Bending his head to avoid cracking his skull on the sloping ceiling, he nudged open the door to the bathroom, glad he'd decided to pay her this overdue visit. He was almost enjoying himself and, for the first time in a very long time, began to think it might be possible to put the past behind him and make a fresh start.

And then she was racing up the stairs after him, calling to him to stop. But she wasn't quite fast enough. He'd already flicked on the light, walked to the old-fashioned sink and seen what it was she'd left on the glass shelf above it.

And he realized it was too late after all. Too late to turn back as she was begging him to do, and too late to plan a future that was free of the past.

Breathless with dismay, Sophie leaned against the doorjamb, one fist pressed to her speeding heart. Her gaze locked with his and she knew without his having to say a word that he'd seen.

No more than a couple of yards separated him from her, yet when he spoke, his words seemed to swim across miles, reaching her ears with that same rushing sense of distance that transmits the human voice halfway around the globe. "This is yours?"

Courage, bravado, defiance—where were they when she most needed them? Huddling in a corner of her mind and leaving her with nothing to speak but the truth! "Yes."

He picked up the package, turned it over in his grimy hand. "It hasn't been opened."

"No. I brought it home only a little while ago, just before you arrived, as a matter of fact." As if that made any difference to the appalling state of affairs!

He nodded and dropped the box back on the shelf, then turned on the hot water and proceeded to scrub his hands, paying particular attention to his short-trimmed nails. When he was done and had hung the towel on the rack, he rebuttoned the cuffs of his shirt.

"Well," he said, impaling her with his cool green gaze, "I imagine you'd like to be alone while you do what has to be done."

"Done?" She felt her face flare with color. Surely he didn't expect . . . ?

His reply made it clear that he did. "Take the test."

"*Now*?"

"Why not now?"

"*You're* here."

The rigid set of his shoulders, the shuttered expression on his face, told her how loath he was to admit the truth of that. "Indeed I am," he said, "and I intend to remain here until we learn the results. I'll be downstairs when you're finished."

She floundered for a reason—any reason—to get rid of him. "What if this . . . procedure . . . has to take place first thing in the morning?"

He picked up the box and read the directions printed on the back. "It doesn't," he said flatly. "It states quite clearly that the test can be administered at any time. So quit stalling and get on with it."

"We're not talking about some mundane matter like— like whether or not a cake's finished baking," she spluttered, embarrassed beyond measure at the situation in which she found herself. "This is something intensely personal and private, and doesn't involve you."

"If your believing you might be pregnant is the result of our having had sex on St. Julian, then it certainly does involve me, Sophie, so take the damn test and put us both out of our misery."

The door clicked shut behind him, cutting off any response she might have felt inclined to make, which was just as well, since realistically, there was nothing she could offer to refute the logic of what he'd said. If she'd thought she had a ghost of a chance of pulling it off, she'd lie to him, tell him the test came out negative. But she'd never been able to look anyone in the eye and tell a barefaced lie. It simply wasn't in her nature. In any case, he was the type who'd ask to see the proof.

She came downstairs fifteen minutes later, but instead of going to where he waited for her, she finished the job she'd started in the kitchen, brewing the coffee and setting mugs, sugar and a jug of cream on a tray, searching out napkins—anything to keep her hands busy and give her mind time to compose itself.

He stood at one of the windows in the living room, staring out at the snow-draped night, but when he heard her come in, he pulled the drapes closed and fastened his attention on her. Acutely conscious of his scrutiny, she set the tray on a low table in front of the fire, which by then was burning brightly.

It was a warm, cosy scene, the kind seen on Christmas cards, with the faded burgundies in her prized antique Turkish carpet echoing the rich red of the velvet curtains. All that was missing was a cat on the hearth and perhaps a smile on the face of the man standing across from her.

"How do you take your coffee?" she asked, trying for a voice that didn't tremble and a smile that didn't waver. Neither quite worked.

"Black," he said. "Did you take the test?"

So much for polite small talk! Abandoning any pretense at gracious hostessing, she replied in the same unadorned vein that he'd asked the question. "Yes."

"And?"

"I'm pregnant." She hadn't expected him to whoop with joy at the news, but his silence bespoke a condemnation that she found insupportable. To end it, she said with a pitiful attempt at irony, "My goodness, is it possible that I've rendered you speechless? Is there nothing you'd like to say to me?"

"Just one thing," he said. "Is the child mine?"

Under different, less strained circumstances, she might have found the question reasonable enough. He was hardly privy to her sexual liaisons after all, and was not to know that, except for a brief affair a long time ago, she'd been intimate with no one until that night on St. Julian. But the way he looked at her when he spoke, as if he'd somehow found himself entangled with a woman of questionable morals, was one thing too much on top of everything else.

Too distraught to hold them back, she let the tears spurt from her eyes and splash down her face. "Yes, it's yours!" she cried. "What do you take me for?"

"Not a virgin, certainly, so please don't try pulling that old chestnut out of the fire."

Already regretting that she hadn't had the wit to answer him with scorching dignity, she drew in a great breath and tried to collect herself. But just when she thought she had the tears under control, she looked at him again and a fresh spate of misery erupted at the empty despair she saw in his eyes. "I've only ever been with one other man and that was when I was twenty-four," she wailed. "Even you can't seriously believe I've been carrying his child for the past three years."

He let fly with a bark of laughter at her response, an incongruous sound in that tension-filled room. "Not quite, no."

Somewhat restored, she swiped at the tears. "I would no more think of trying to pass off another man's child than I would—"

"There's no need to belabor the point, Sophie. I believed you the first time you said the child was mine." Finally abandoning his post by the window, he came over and dropped into the chair opposite hers. Elbows braced on his knees and hands dangling limply, he went on, "What we must now decide is how to proceed from here."

He was going to offer her money, put forth options that she'd find unacceptable. She could sense it in the way he hesitated as though anxious to phrase his idea as delicately as possible. "I will not have an abortion," she said flatly, forestalling the suggestion before he aired it.

He raised his eyebrows reproachfully. "Have I suggested you should?"

"Not yet, but you were about to. I can tell."

"It would be as well if you didn't try to second-guess me, Sophie, particularly since you do it so badly. An abortion is the last thing I have in mind." He picked up his mug of coffee and took a mouthful. "The way I see it, there's only one course of action open to us. We'll get married as soon as it can be arranged."

"*Married*?"

He misunderstood the dismay she couldn't hide. "I know your career is important to you and that having a child right now is probably at the bottom of your list of priorities." He shrugged and stared into the fire. "For what it's worth, it's not exactly number one on mine, either."

Should she tell him that her dearest ambition was not to go down in history as the most illustrious water-garden artist of the modern world, but to settle down with a good man and have babies? But that not in her worst nightmare had she imagined it happening like this, with a coldly proposed merger between the future parents of a child carelessly conceived while the father was in grief for his true, lost love?

"If the idea of marrying me is so very repulsive to you, Sophie," he said, breaking into her reverie, "think of it as a temporary solution. We'll stay together for two years and then evaluate the situation. By then, the difficult early months of late-night feedings and colic and all those other things that babies apparently thrive on, will be over. We'll both have had time to adjust to the idea of parenthood and at least we'll know we gave our child the best possible start in life, with two parents who put his welfare before their own."

He smiled, a wry, sad curving of his sexy mouth, as though he knew very well that what he was about to say next was highly unlikely. "And who knows, maybe we'll find we manage rather well together, and a divorce won't be worth the inconvenience and upheaval it will create. Stranger things have been known to happen, you know, and perhaps our chances are better than average since neither of us is dazzled by notions of romantic happily-ever-after. This is a match made in bed, not heaven, and I think we're both too intelligent not to recognize that.''

In her secret heart, Sophie knew that, had they met under other circumstances, their relationship might have evolved differently and they might have found happiness together. Now he'd flung the opportunity into her lap and she knew only an overwhelming sadness because clearly he expected no such outcome.

"You seem to have thought of every angle except one,'' she said bleakly. "What are people going to think of our getting married so soon after Barbara's death?''

"I stopped caring what other people think a long time ago.''

"I didn't. And whether you want to admit it or not, there are some who would be hurt if we were to go ahead as you suggest. The Wexlers, for instance. They're finding it difficult enough to cope with losing a daughter without finding they're losing the son they almost had, as well.''

He stared into the fire again and she thought how hard he looked at times, how much like one of his bulldozers flattening everything standing in its way. "That part of my life is over as Gail and John Wexler will be the first to understand,'' he said. "Any other obstacles you'd like to throw up?''

Just one, but she wasn't fool enough to invite his scorn by giving voice to it. Of all the reasons he'd listed for them to marry, he hadn't once mentioned love, and if she was idiot enough to want gilt on her gingerbread, he didn't have to be made aware of the fact.

"I can't think of any, not at the moment."

"Well, then?" He fixed her in his laser-sharp gaze. "What's your answer? Are we engaged, or not?"

CHAPTER FOUR

OF COURSE she and Dominic Winter weren't engaged! The question was preposterous. They were on the brink of the twenty-first century, for heaven's sake, and shotgun weddings had gone out of fashion a long time ago, along with marriages of convenience.

On top of that, he didn't much like her. No man who proposed marriage in such cut-and-dried terms could possibly harbor any fondness for his intended bride. And although she might find him scandalously appealing, Sophie wasn't so far in thrall to the attraction that she was willing to sacrifice herself on the altar of conventionality because she happened to be carrying his baby.

"Well, Sophie? What's your answer? Are you going to marry me?"

She studied his well-shaped head with its sweep of thick black hair, and the equally dark parentheses of his brows. She hazarded a glance into those still green eyes, found it a thoroughly unnerving experience and quickly passed on to his very sexy mouth.

A terrible mistake! Desire, plain and simple, stabbed her, laying waste to what was left of her meager supply of common sense. If she'd dared close her own eyes, she knew her mind would have been filled with memories of St. Julian. Of the heady perfume of flowers and the rhythmic roll of the surf. And of Dominic lying naked beside her, all smooth, firm muscle and sleek, silken strength. The possibility, however slim, of that same sweet rush of passion consuming her again, of its weaving an indelible thread through the fabric of her life, seduced her into what she could only assume constituted temporary insanity.

Her mouth formed a reply without any regard for the frantic message from her brain. "All right, we'll give it a try."

He rubbed his hands together with the brisk satisfaction of a man who'd just effected a contract so full of loopholes through which he could extricate himself that he didn't have to worry about the problems inherent in its execution. "Good. What sort of wedding would you like? A traditional affair with all the trappings—" he let his glance slide fleetingly to her still-slender waist "—or something more discreet?"

Scrambling to gather her scattered wits, she said, "Right now, I'm more concerned about our reaching a clear understanding of the kind of marriage we're entering into than I am about the social correctness of my having a white wedding."

"I'm not sure I know what you mean."

"Well, this isn't exactly the customary way to go about things."

He inclined his head in assent. "I thought we'd already agreed that it's not."

"Yes," she said, "we have."

"Then what is it you don't understand?"

She might have known he'd make her spell it out. "What do you want of me in all this, Dominic? What sort of living arrangements do you have in mind?"

"Are you talking about sex, Sophie?"

A blush chased all the way up from her feet to her face. "I'm trying to discuss a delicate subject without causing either of us unnecessary embarrassment, something which you're obviously incapable of appreciating."

"You *are* talking about sex." A hint of glee touched his mouth but was gone before it had time to reach his eyes. "If I was not prepared to honor my obligations to you, I would not have proposed marriage. The same code of decency forbids my demanding conjugal rights from an unwilling wife. Whether or not we share the same bed is entirely up to you, Sophie. I am perfectly willing to follow your lead."

"You—you're making this very difficult," she stammered.

"Not at all. I'm not made of stone, nor am I immune to your considerable charms—witness the fact that you conceived my baby in a thoroughly orthodox fashion. If you want me again—for whatever reason—all you have to do is let me know. We're both normal, healthy people, subject to normal, healthy urges, and I can't imagine that either of us will jump to any farfetched conclusions in the event that we choose to satisfy them. Does that clarify matters for you?"

Dear Lord, yes! In spades! He would marry her and even enjoy sex with her, but he would not love her.

"I see that I have." He stood up and flexed his shoulders, a gesture Sophie found herself watching with morbid fascination. "It's been a long day. Why don't we table further discussion until tomorrow?"

It was probably the only smart suggestion he'd made all night. Sophie needed to be alone. More than anything, she needed to climb into bed and sleep the clock around, and hope that that would be enough to restore her sanity.

And then she could do what she should have done tonight: say "Thank you very much, Dominic, but I won't marry you although I do appreciate your having asked.'' She'd do it now if she wasn't so desperately tired and he wasn't so hard to say no to.

He touched her face, running the back of his fingers from her jaw to her cheekbone. ''I have a meeting with my architect at nine in the morning, and another with my project manager right after,'' he said, ''but I should be finished by noon. What say we get together for lunch some time after that, and you can tell me what you've decided on in the way of a wedding? And then, perhaps, we should break the news to your family. I imagine they'd like to hear it before it becomes common knowledge around town.''

The mere thought of her parents' shock and surprise at learning their daughter was rushing headlong into marriage with a stranger almost had Sophie doing the brave and decent thing and saying right there and then that she couldn't continue playing this charade a moment longer. But there was something so invincible in the set of Dominic's spectacular shoulders, in the unwavering gaze of his long-lashed green eyes, that she took refuge in cowardice once again.

''I suppose so,'' she hedged, disgusted by the pitifully indecisive creature she'd become.

Her tone, or perhaps the way she fairly drooped with exhaustion, had Dominic subjecting her to an even more thorough scrutiny. ''You look worn out,'' he said, the concern in his words seriously eroding her composure.

''I feel worn out,'' she practically whimpered.

''Then go to bed and get some rest.'' He leaned forward and surprised her with a kiss full on her mouth. It was brief and hard and dismayingly arousing. ''Good night, Sophie. Sleep well and I'll see you tomorrow.''

She had an early appointment herself the next morning, a consultation for a fountain garden in the atrium of one of Palmerstown's grand old houses, which was being turned into apartments. Although she always made a point of looking her best for such meetings, Sophie spent extra time that day, applying more makeup than she usually wore, in an attempt to camouflage the ravages of fatigue. Because, Dominic's exhortation notwithstanding, she had not slept the previous night, let alone slept well. Her mind had been too full of the man whose impact on her life had her swinging repeatedly from resentment to desire, from simple logic to wild fantasy.

What if she married him and things did work out between them? she'd wondered as midnight crept past. What if they fell in love after the fact instead of before? It wasn't unheard of after all, and their one experience of intimacy had been breathtaking, at least for her. Why couldn't it always be that way? Why couldn't something strong and enduring grow out of the passion and closeness that came from lovemaking?

But then the pendulum swung the other way, stripping her dreams of their magic and revealing them for the foolish delusions they were. A man like Dominic Winter wasn't the type to switch allegiance so quickly. He had loved Barbara and was still grieving her death. Sophie was merely an inconvenience he'd brought upon himself during a moment of weakness, one for which he was paying the price.

For him, it had been sex, careless sex: something that never would have happened had he not been so tormented by his loss. But happen it had, and since he no longer had a future with Barbara, he was doing the honorable thing by the woman who had briefly brought him surcease from his pain. If truth be known, he probably had to think twice to remember Sophie's name.

And so it went, back and forth, until the cold light of reason, coinciding with that of morning, finally won out. She was twenty-seven, not seventeen, and had too much pride to run second best with any man, even if he was the father of her child.

She chose her wardrobe with care: a wool dress with a dropped waist and flared skirt, simple gold jewelry and plain black leather accessories. The ensemble boosted her confidence just an extra notch because she didn't delude herself. Rejecting Dominic wasn't going to be easy.

She did briefly entertain the thought that he, too, might have had second thoughts and decided to call the whole affair off. It seemed unlikely, however, especially when she checked her answering service about ten-thirty and learned that he'd made a one o'clock lunch reservation in the Lakeside Room at the Royal Hotel. A person didn't need to go to such lavish lengths to end things, especially not when a simple phone call would do the job just as well. She very much feared that, as far as Dominic was concerned, the engagement was still on.

Being kept waiting left Dominic in a very testy frame of mind. Admittedly, it wasn't her fault that he got to the hotel ten minutes early, but that didn't prevent his irritation from growing when she still hadn't shown up at five past one.

He dismissed the notion that her nonappearance might be an indication that she'd had second thoughts about marrying him. If she thought that by standing him up she'd so easily slither off the matrimonial hook, she sadly underestimated him. At the very least, he expected the courtesy of a face-to-face refusal. And in this case, a refusal wasn't an option he was prepared to accept.

Forcing himself not to look at his watch again, he thumbed through the morning paper to the business section and immersed himself in the stock market report. Too bad women weren't as easy to analyze!

Granted, she'd looked a bit thunderstruck last night when he'd come out with his proposal and he supposed, to be fair, that he might have employed a little more finesse, but hell, she wasn't the only one reeling with shock. Just when, if ever, she'd planned to let him in on her little secret, had he not shown up when he did, was something he'd never know. The point was, as soon as he'd found out she was pregnant, there'd only ever been one outcome for the two of them and that was marriage.

It might not be the ideal solution but, the way he saw it, they could both do worse. He was going on thirty-six, experienced enough to know women weren't repelled by him, and smart enough to know that it took a lot more than illusions of love to make a marriage work. Furthermore, he'd meant what he said about a child needing two full-time parents. Weekend daddy was not a role he'd willingly adopt.

And she?

He flipped the page irritably. Hell, by her own admission she was no sexual ingenue. She knew how babies were made and if she hadn't wanted to be saddled with a child, she should have kept her distance, instead of seducing him with sympathy.

Her familiar white car screeching to a stop outside the hotel's front entrance diverted his attention. The driver's door swung wide on its hinges, a daintily shod foot emerged, a flare of teal blue fabric swirled around a well-turned ankle. Pale gold hair spilled over the collar of a winter white cape, a head turned, a smile captivated the doorman into whistling for the parking attendant.

She smiled again and, gathering the collar of her cape close at her throat, hooked a black handbag over her wrist and reached out a gloved hand to set the hotel's revolving brass doors in motion.

To his intense annoyance, Dominic felt his mouth go dry.

The Royal was the most splendid among Palmerstown's admittedly few hotels, but that was not to say it lagged behind its big-city counterparts. Its old-world opulence and dignity rendered it beyond question the only place in town with the glamour and panache to host special occasions. Weddings, anniversaries, charity balls, it knew them all.

Sophie, though, had always found its Austrian chandeliers and extravagantly molded ceilings rather formidable. Even the views of Jewel Lake from its tall, elegant windows were overwhelming. However, it was the sort of place that suited Dominic Winter to a T— big, impressive, invincible.

The minute she entered the foyer shortly before a quarter past one, she saw him. He leaned against one of the ornately carved library tables, scanning the morning paper and looking as he always did: well dressed and supremely at ease with himself and his place in the greater scheme of things. No one would have guessed he'd found out, just the night before, that he had fathered a child with a woman he barely knew.

"Sorry I'm a bit late," she said, slightly out of breath more from nerves than exertion. "I had rather a full morning."

He pushed away from the table and cast a pointed glance at the grandfather clock in the corner. "Did you?

Well, the next time you decide to keep me waiting, do me the courtesy of phoning and letting me know in advance.''

She refrained from telling him there and then that there wasn't going to be a "next time", at least not in the way he thought, and said only, "Sorry, it couldn't be helped."

Of course, he couldn't just leave well enough alone. He looked down at her from his lofty height and said patronizingly, "Time is money in the business world, you know, and I have little patience with people unwilling to appreciate that."

"I'll keep that in mind," she retorted, her own hackles only too ready to rise in retaliation, "provided you do me the courtesy of remembering that I'm in business, too, and it just so happens I had a previously scheduled appointment across town that took up most of my morning. As it is, I had to cut things short to get here when I did."

"Humph," he snorted. "Well, now that you are here, let's get a move on. We have a great deal to discuss."

Slapping the newspaper down on the table, he relieved her of her cape and deposited it in the coat-check booth. At about the same time, a burst of laughter erupted from the Lakeside Room, followed seconds later by a group of women who streamed across the carpeted foyer toward the revolving doors.

Striding back toward her, Dominic took Sophie by the elbow and drew her aside to let them pass unimpeded. Perhaps if he hadn't, they might have flowed around her, too involved in their animated conversation to take note of the rather ordinary woman busy scooping her hair free of her dress collar.

But no matter what their age, Dominic Winter was too arresting a man for women to overlook, especially when they were a little giddy from a celebration lunch. And most especially when they belatedly recognized the person he was escorting and saw the way he held on to her as if he had the right, as if, like a parcel of land, she was something he owned.

"Why, look, Anne!" one of them caroled. "Here's Sophie, come to check up on her mother!"

Sophie stood rooted to the spot, appalled to find herself and Dominic the object of mass curiosity. Eight pairs of eyes darted birdlike from her face to his and back again as the chatter, which moments before had filled the lobby, sank into expectant silence.

Her mother was the one to break it. "Hello, dear!" she exclaimed. "What a nice surprise running into you like this!"

She didn't add, *With this interesting, handsome man and when are you going to remember your manners and introduce us*? but she might as well have done. Neither her attention nor that of her friends faltered by so much as a blink.

"Um..." Sophie muttered inarticulately. "Um... Mom...?"

Anne Casson's gaze flitted to Dominic again. "That's right, dear," she said encouragingly. "What brings you here in the middle of the working day?"

"I'm...um, we're...having lunch."

"Oh, so were we," her mother chirped. "Our annual Valentine's Day lunch. You know the ladies from my bridge club, don't you?"

"Yes," Sophie mumbled, continuing to behave like a socially arrested teenager. Miserably aware of Dominic looming at her side, she faced up to the unavoidable. "And this...um, this is..."

"Dominic Winter." The scowl provoked by Sophie's late arrival melted beneath the warmth of the smile he turned on her mother. "How do you do, Mrs. Casson? I'm delighted to meet you."

Anne Casson never had had much of a head for wine. One glass stretched her tolerance practically to the limit. Sophie could only suppose she'd had two that day. How else to account for the outrageous liberties she proceeded to take?

Simpering at Dominic, who was busy doling out more charm than he'd ever spared Sophie in all the weeks she'd sort of known him, her mother said, "I'm very pleased to meet you, too, Mr. Winter," then had the nerve to add coyly, "Have you and my daughter been friends for very long?"

"Long enough for me to ask her to marry me and for her to accept," he announced baldly.

The mingled gasps and squeals *that* elicited from his audience quite swallowed up Sophie's groan of dismay.

"Marry? Oh, my dear, what wonderful news!" Wreathed in smiles, Anne folded Sophie in a hug. "When did all this happen?"

"Last night, which is why you weren't informed sooner," Dominic said, speaking for both of them as if Sophie's tongue had taken a walk. "We're hoping to fine-tune the arrangements over lunch."

Sophie's mother dimpled disgustingly. "Then I won't detain you, but won't you both please come for dinner this evening? I know my husband is going to be as thrilled with your news as I am, and he'll certainly want to meet the man his daughter's agreed to marry."

"We'd be delighted, wouldn't we, Sophie?" Dominic said, his perfunctory invitation for her opinion nothing more than token acknowledgment that she understood English.

"Well, actually—"

"Shall we say around seven?" her mother cut in, apparently no more concerned with her daughter's views than he was.

Placing his hand in the small of Sophie's back and steering her firmly toward the dining room, Dominic nodded. "Perfect," he allowed.

Resisting the urge to drag her feet like a reluctant child, Sophie followed the hostess to the best table in the room. Set in a vaulted alcove overlooking the lake and secluded from other diners by marble pillars and a screen of tropical plants, it was the ideal spot to bill and coo— or engage in outright warfare.

Sophie chose the latter. "What did you do that for?" she demanded crossly as soon as they were alone.

Dominic picked up the menu and perused it at leisure before deigning to inquire, "Do what?"

"You know perfectly well what! Going on about our being engaged, as if it was a fait accompli."

"But it is, Sophie," he said flatly, regarding her over the top of the menu. "Make no mistake about that."

"Don't be ridiculous! You don't really want to marry me. The only reason you even suggested it is because you feel responsible for me and—"

"That's not why," he said.

The remark, dropped so coolly in the face of her simmering outrage, threw her into total confusion. "It's *not*?"

"Not in the slightest."

Offended despite herself, Sophie glared at him. "Then what is?"

"The child, of course. I thought we agreed last night that you and I—what we want, what we had planned—aren't what matter here," he said, his voice chill with reproof. "I am marrying you to give our child a name."

"It will have a name," she said. "Mine."

"And a few others, too, if you have your way, including 'bastard'."

"Dominic, people don't think like that anymore. In this day and age, it doesn't make any difference if a child has only one parent."

He ignored her. Or at least, he ignored her for a moment and turned his attention to the waiter discreetly hovering beyond the pillars. Only after he'd ordered a scotch for himself and a Perrier with lime for her did he resume the conversation.

"A child never has only one parent," he pronounced, leaning back in his chair and pinning her in his sharp, intelligent gaze, "although some unfortunate children might never know more than one. Mine, however, will not be among that number."

"I wasn't suggesting cutting you out of our baby's life," Sophie exclaimed, wondering why on earth she was arguing the point with him when, logic and wisdom notwithstanding, part of her yearned simply to give in. It had always been like that where he was concerned: balancing precariously on the knife-edge of emotion, with pulsing attraction ready to engulf her on one side, and on the other its antidote, hostility.

Even at his most imperious, he was still attractive, and she wished he'd found something in his undoubtedly extensive wardrobe other than the tailored camel-hair jacket and ivory shirt that set off his tanned skin and dark hair to such advantage.

She sighed, last night's inner war breaking out anew and raging as fiercely as ever without either side showing signs of gaining the upper hand. "We don't have to get married for you to play a part in his or her upbringing," she said, clinging to reason despite the insidious little voice within trying to sabotage her efforts.

Dominic continued to regard her impassively. At length, he said, "All right. We won't."

The most dreadful, contrary disappointment welled up and struck her solidly in the solar plexus. "We won't?" she echoed.

He shook his head and smiled with suspect affability. "No. Since you find the idea so offensive, I'm perfectly willing to bring up the child by myself."

"*Without me*?" Outrage combined with astonishment to send her voice soaring.

"Of course not. To quote you, I'm not suggesting cutting you out of our baby's life, but we don't have to be married for you to play a part in his or her upbringing."

"But it's my baby! I'm its mother!"

"It's my baby, too," he countered with irrefutable logic. "I'm its father."

"What are you hinting at, Dominic?"

"Hinting?" He laughed scornfully. "I'm not hinting, Sophie. I'm *telling* you that I'll assume full custody of our child and accord you generous visitation rights."

She hadn't expected he'd make things easy for her but never in her wildest imaginings had she anticipated this! "A man alone bringing up a baby?" she scoffed, sounding a lot more certain than she really felt. "It'll never happen!"

"You're wrong." He spoke calmly and with utter, inflexible finality. "It's a not uncommon arrangement these days. As you've pointed out, we're living in the nineties. Single fathers are finally receiving their due and being acknowledged as having the same rights as single mothers to the full pleasures of parenthood. They no longer have to assume the role of powerless spectators in the raising of their children."

"You'll never persuade the courts to see things that way. You won't be able to coerce a judge the way you're trying to pressure me."

"I won't have to. I'll simply provide an excellent home, hire a nanny of unimpeachable reputation and a house-keeper and, if necessary, the best possible legal represen-tation to be had—none of which you can afford to do. I'm sure, given all that, that a judge would be quite happy to award me custody."

"This isn't about money, Dominic!" she whispered furiously. "You can't buy a child."

"Of course you can, Sophie," he purred with a shameful lack of guilt. "Anything can be bought for a price, including a judge, provided a person has enough money—and I do."

"You're bluffing."

He leaned forward as though what he had to impart next was of the utmost confidentiality. "You don't know me very well. If you did, you'd recognize that I'm very single-minded once I decide to go after something. I don't give up and I don't back down as more than a few people in this town who've tried to cross me can attest. I can count on one hand those who've succeeded, Sophie, and still have five fingers left at the end of the exercise."

He was the most despicable man she'd ever known. Yet although the blood raced through her veins at twice its normal speed, heating her cheeks and sending per-spiration prickling down her spine, something cold and fearful lodged in Sophie's heart. "I will never give up my baby."

"Then you'll have to marry me because those are the only two choices you have."

It was what some aberrant streak in her had wanted all along, to be left with no alternative but to marry him. That way she wouldn't have to deal with all the uncertainties that nagged at her. Instead, she could consign herself to destiny in the shape of Dominic Winter. "Go with the flow", as Elaine was fond of saying. And bend all her energies to creating something wonderful out of something improbable, love and happiness out of carelessness and inconvenience.

But not this way. Not because he was blackmailing or intimidating her.

Suddenly, she hated him. Hated his imperturbable confidence, his certainty that he would win no matter what obstacles she threw in his path. Hated his smoldering sex appeal, the graceful fingers curled so casually around his glass, the long, dark lashes drawn down to cover the expression in his eyes. The empty, beautiful smile on his cruel, beautiful mouth.

"Then I will marry you, and I will make your life a living hell," she promised rashly, tears trembling in her voice.

He stretched out both his hands and pried apart her clenched fists, stroking each finger with a tenderness that, at any previous time in their association, would have reduced her to putty. But not now. Never again, after today.

"Will you?" he asked softly.

"Yes," she said, wrenching her fingers free. "I will. *I will*, Dominic."

He raised his lashes and bathed her in the cool green depths of his gaze. "No, you won't, my darling. Because that will not be a healthy environment for our child and you will want the very best for him."

"Her," she said mutinously. She didn't want a son. Sons grew up into power-hungry men with no heart.

"Her," he conceded, waxing magnanimous. "So, are there any more objections, or are we once again agreed that marriage is the best resolution of our situation?"

"What if I try hard to make it work and despite that you're dreadfully unhappy with me?" she said, snatching to find straws and finding them pathetically thin on the ground.

His laughter rang out, a rich blend of amusement and exasperation. "Don't you know that if you go looking for trouble, you're certain to find it?"

"But we're not in love," she said, finally finding the courage to bare what to her was the fatal flaw in their arrangement.

He sobered. "No, we're not. And as I pointed out last night, that improves our chances of making a success of things. When you have few expectations, you're less likely to be disappointed."

Oh, she really did hate him! At this rate, she'd probably murder him before the ink was dry on the marriage license!

She cast about for something with which to puncture his self-confidence, to make him question, just a little, his invincibility. "Is this the way you went about things with Barbara, railroading her into a marriage she didn't want? Is that why she felt she had to get away from you?" she asked flippantly. And immediately regretted having done so.

His face wiped itself clean of all expression. Only his eyes glowed with a light that was almost feral. "My relationship with Barbara is none of your business and I have no intention of discussing it or her with you."

The pain Sophie had sought to inflict turned itself on her with brutal force. How foolish of her to have thought she could hurt him! There was nothing she could do that would matter to him, neither love him nor hate him, because he didn't care. He was too numb to feel anything she leveled his way.

Everything sweet he had to give to a woman, he'd given to Barbara. All that he had left for Sophie was his bitterness at having lost the real love of his life.

If she were truly vindictive, she would increase his misery a thousandfold. She would tell him how his fiancée had betrayed him during her fling on St. Julian. She would reduce him to the same despair that he'd invoked in her.

But she could never hurt him like that no matter how richly he deserved it. Because, of course, she could never really hate him no matter how much she wished she could.

CHAPTER FIVE

HE HAD to know he'd won. Even a fool could have interpreted the body language so clearly trumpeted by the slump in her spine, the trembling in her hands, the way she bent her head so that her hair fell forward to hide the distress on her face. And whatever else he might be, Dominic was no fool.

"You'll feel better when you've eaten," he announced blandly, nudging the menu toward her.

She would be sick all over the table if she took so much as a mouthful of food. And it would serve him right! "I'm not hungry."

"Well, I didn't say you were, Sophie," he replied, all sunny equanimity now that he'd wrung surrender out of her. "I said—"

"I heard what you said! Every last, extorting word!"

"*Extorting*?" Laughter untouched by anything but genuine entertainment came weaving across the table to filter its way through the strands of her hair.

"Enjoy your amusement, Dominic," she snapped, staring at the carpet and refusing to be coaxed into forgiving him. "It won't last long."

"Ahem," the waiter said, and Sophie saw his well-polished black shoes come to a halt beside her.

"My fiancée will have the cream of asparagus soup, followed by a small portion of sole," Dominic decreed, laughter still shimmering in his voice, "but I'll settle for something a bit more fortifying. Bring me a spinach salad and the oyster stew."

78

When it was placed in front of her, Sophie wanted to throw the soup all over him. It would have afforded her delicious pleasure to watch the rich green cream drooling down his expensive camel-hair jacket. But the aroma of delicate herbs and fresh asparagus was too tempting and she wished she'd not told him she wasn't hungry. Doing her best to pretend he wasn't there, she spooned a little of the soup into her mouth.

"How is it?" he asked.

She touched her napkin to her lips. "Excellent, thank you."

"Good. You need to look after yourself."

One word about my eating for two, she thought savagely, *and he really will be wearing this*! "I'm not in the habit of doing otherwise."

"Have you been bothered by morning sickness?"

"A little, when I first get out of bed, but it doesn't last long."

"Have you seen a doctor?"

"No, Dominic," she said, staring at her soup because anything was preferable to looking at him in his present solicitous mood. "I just told you, I'm feeling very well."

"Nevertheless, pregnant women shouldn't take any chances. I know a very good obstetrician—"

"So do I," she said shortly.

"Then make an appointment, Sophie, and let me know the date and time."

"Whatever for?"

"Because I intend to go with you for the first visit."

Her spoon fell into her soup with a decided clatter. "Absolutely not!" she said flatly, abandoning her study of the tabletop and favoring him with a glare. "If you think I'm about to have you...let you..."

"What?" He raised quizzical brows.

Witness me flat on my back, with my ankles hoisted into stirrups and heaven only knows how much of me on display . . .! Her face flamed, giving her away.

Of course, he noticed. He noticed everything he wasn't supposed to see, from pregnancy tests to the precise number of seconds he'd been kept waiting for his blasted lunch.

"Oh, for Pete's sake, Sophie, I'm not suggesting I accompany you into the examining room!" he snorted. "I'm no voyeur. If I'm going to see you naked, I'd just as soon do so in private. All I want is to talk to the doctor and find out what I can do to make the pregnancy as pleasant as possible for you."

Just when she'd decided he lacked a single redeeming quality, he came out with something that left her feeling smutty-minded and immature. Grudgingly, she muttered, "Well . . . thank you."

"You're welcome," he said. "Now can we call a truce and concentrate on enjoying this excellent lunch?"

Somehow she managed, resorting to monosyllabic answers to his attempts at general conversation. But there was one subject she felt obliged to discuss more thoroughly before they went their separate ways for the afternoon.

"About our having dinner this evening with my parents," she said. "You might as well be prepared for the fact that you won't bamboozle my father as easily as you did my mother. She's been itching to be mother of the bride ever since my brother got married and all she got to do was cry at the ceremony. My father's a different proposition altogether. He's likely to ask some very awkward questions."

"I'll be happy to answer them," Dominic said calmly.

"No doubt. The point is, I'm not sure how much we should tell them—about the baby, that is."

"I'm not afraid to come out with the truth, if that's what's worrying you. On the other hand, our reasons aren't anyone else's business but our own, so if you'd rather your parents didn't know about the pregnancy, that's how we'll handle it."

"I hate deceiving them but in this case I think it might be best if we don't share everything with them, not yet at least. I'm afraid they'll jump to all the right conclusions if we do, and that would worry them terribly."

"What conclusions are you referring to, Sophie?"

"The fact that we barely know each other and aren't the least bit in love."

He smiled wryly. "I see. Then we'll keep quiet and put on an act that will convince them otherwise."

"What about your parents?"

"Parent," he corrected her. "And he isn't interested in my doings."

Curiosity begged to be satisfied but it was clear from the way that mask of privacy suddenly descended over Dominic's features that the subject of his family, like that of Barbara, was closed.

"If I don't know anything about you," Sophie ventured, "how am I ever going to convince anyone that I want to marry you? It isn't normal for people not to talk about their families. For instance, have I mentioned that I'm a twin, or that my brother is seventeen minutes older than I am and presently living with his wife in England, completing a research fellowship in Roman history?"

"Good God!" Dominic exclaimed, for the first time looking faintly rattled. "Does that mean you might give birth to twins, as well?"

"Not necessarily. At least, I don't think so. But that's not the point."

He shot back his cuff and checked the time on his watch. "You're quite right, it's not," he agreed, scribbling his signature on the bill and pocketing his credit card. "Unfortunately, I can't take the time to exchange personal histories right now. I have a meeting with the land development office at city hall, so I'm afraid the sordid story of my life will have to wait."

She barely had the chance to collect her purse and gloves before he was ushering her out of the dining room and into the foyer. He retrieved her cape and sent the parking valet scurrying for their cars.

"Where shall we meet tonight?" she asked as he hustled her toward the revolving doors.

"We won't," he said. "I'll pick you up at six-thirty. That should give us enough time, shouldn't it?"

To get to her parents' home by seven, perhaps, but not to fill in all the biographical blanks. She grabbed at his sleeve in an attempt to slow him down. "Dominic, I think we need a bit longer than that. Can you make it half past five instead, so that we can talk about...well, things we need to learn about each other?"

Impatiently, he swung back to face her. "No. I hear what you're saying, and once again I admit you're right, but it's something that will have to wait."

"I see." She blew out a sigh. "Well, I can't very well force you to tell me things you don't want me to know. But sooner or later, you're going to have to make a few concessions, or this marriage we're contemplating really will be pure hell whether you like it or not. You can't expect me to be the one who always backs down. I'm not cut out to be any man's doormat."

"It never occurred to me that you were. On the other hand, if you hadn't been so bloody-minded about trying to wriggle out of marrying me, we could have spent the past hour discussing the very things you're harping on about. Now I really have to get a move on. Have a nice afternoon."

Talk about being summarily dismissed! Resentfully, Sophie watched his long-legged stride carry him outside and into the black Jaguar, and decided that they were in for a very rough ride indeed if this was how he intended to approach their marriage.

Her mother had gone to considerable trouble to make the evening festive. She'd put champagne on ice, and candles and bowls of flowers were everywhere in the apartment: tulips and freesia on the living room coffee table, roses in the dining alcove, and even a little crystal vase of Devon violets in the powder room.

Her father, although warm enough in his greeting, seemed a little more reserved in his pleasure. "So this is the man who's swept my daughter off her feet," he remarked, sizing Dominic up. "Well, although I must congratulate you on your good taste, I admit I'm a bit bowled over. It strikes me you've arrived at this decision rather suddenly."

The beginnings of a blush warmed Sophie's cheeks. Aware of her father's glance swinging toward her, she busied herself helping her mother pass around slender flutes of champagne.

"I think I took Sophie by surprise, too," Dominic agreed, neatly evading any sort of explanation for the unexpectedness of his proposal. "But when the time is right, there's not much point in postponing, is there?"

"As long as you're both sure you know what you're doing, I suppose not," her father admitted doubtfully.

"Sophie's old enough to make up her own mind, and it's not as if there's any big rush to set a wedding date."

The flush that Sophie had just about brought under control flared up again. Noticing, Dominic relieved her of the glass she was about to offer him and slid an arm around her shoulders. "Call me an anxious bridegroom if you like, Mr. Casson, but I don't want to wait a day longer than I have to to make Sophie my wife," he said, gazing with every appearance of besotted adoration into her eyes.

"I see," her father said, plainly not seeing at all. "So when's it going to be, Sophie?"

She would have loved to land Dominic in the thick of things and say, *Don't ask me. I'm only the bride and haven't been told yet*, but all that would have done was worry her parents. "Well," she hedged, "we...um, we thought some time around...um..."

"The first Saturday in March," Dominic supplied.

Her mother gasped. "But that's less than four weeks away!"

Sophie saw the sharpened speculation in her father's eyes and her cheeks burned. She swallowed twice, knowing full well she looked like a guilty child found with her fingers in the cookie jar.

Dominic noticed and immediately took steps to effect a little damage control. Shielding her with his body, he bent his head and brought his mouth down on hers. It was a very calculated kiss, not too long, not too short, and appropriately enthusiastic.

It might have been tolerable if he'd closed his eyes for the duration, but he didn't. He kept them wide open and stared at her. She knew because she stared right back. It was her only defense against the disconcerting urge to melt into his embrace and pretend the kiss was for real.

With the possible exception of Sophie's father, no one could have guessed that the prospective bride and groom were anything but panting to exchange their vows and plunge into happily-ever-after.

Her mother burst into tears. "I'm so happy for the two of you," she sobbed cheerfully.

But her father, still plainly suspicious of the whole endeavor, said, "I thought weddings took a long time to plan. Is there anything else you'd like to tell us while you're at it?"

Keeping Sophie firmly within the protection of his arm, Dominic shook his head. "Not at this time, sir," he replied with a firmness that brooked no further interrogation.

"Well," Doug Casson conceded, backing down, "as long as you're happy, Sophie."

"I am," Sophie muttered, doing her damnedest to look radiant.

Mercifully, her mother produced a notepad and shifted the focus to the practical arrangements of putting together a wedding on such short notice. Over the course of dinner, it was settled that the church ceremony would be followed by a small but elegant wedding breakfast in the Crystal Room at the Royal, followed by a brief honeymoon whose destination had yet to be decided.

"Spring's a busy time of year in my business," Dominic explained. "I'm afraid I can't afford to take off more than a few days."

For the first time since they'd arrived, Sophie's father showed some real enthusiasm for the topic under discussion. "I've read about your company and understand you run an impressive operation, Dominic. Residential construction, isn't it?"

Dominic nodded. "With the emphasis on low-density housing. I'm not one of those developers whose first priority is to chop up a piece of land into as many building lots as is legally possible."

At last a safe subject, Sophie thought gratefully, but her relief faded as quickly as it had arisen when her father remarked, "Well, Sophie only just got back from a holiday in the Caribbean, so I don't suppose she'll mind postponing the honeymoon."

"Oh, let's not talk about that," her mother said. "Every time I think of that poor young woman drowning...! Of course, you must know all about that, Dominic. It was in all the papers and—"

Not daring to cast a glance in Dominic's direction, Sophie braced herself for the worst.

Dear heaven, it was all going to come out, she thought in horror. Her father, whose memory would put an elephant's to shame, would recall every last detail that was printed or aired about Barbara Wexler's death. He'd put two and two together and come up with a big, fat four, and this supposed engagement celebration would be exposed for the shabby little deception it really was.

But she had not counted on Dominic, who cut her mother off before she could elaborate further. "Yes, it was tragic," he said impassively. "Have we covered everything to do with the wedding, do you think?"

"The dress!" Instantly diverted, Anne Casson scribbled frantically on her notepad. "If you're thinking of white, we'll have to get going on it immediately, Sophie, although you could probably find something from the sample rack that could be altered to fit if you had to." She eyed Sophie assessingly. "You're still a size eight, dear, aren't you?"

Sophie shot a beseeching glance at Dominic. "She was when we met," he said, for once seeming to be at a loss for the right answer.

"And when was that?" her father wanted to know.

While Dominic skated over the thin ice of judicious truth, Sophie tried not to choke on her mother's excellent chicken Marsala. By the time the evening dragged to a close, she was a nervous wreck.

"That," she groaned, the minute they drove away from her parents' building, "was a nightmare. I don't know how I managed to get through it. When the subject of Bar—um, the Caribbean came up, I was horribly afraid they'd connect you with . . . the whole thing."

"That was over two months ago," Dominic said. "People soon forget—at least, most do."

But not you, Sophie thought bleakly. *You'll never forget.*

"It was a bit like tap-dancing through a mine field, though," he went on. "Lies of omission require some pretty fancy footwork."

She stared at the dim outline of his profile illuminated in the lights from the dashboard. "Yet you managed very well."

"That came out sounding like an accusation, Sophie, as if you think I make a career out of withholding the truth from people."

"Do you?"

"Only when it's absolutely necessary."

"Does that mean that you'll lie to me if I persist with questions you don't want to answer?"

"I'd prefer to be completely straightforward with you, but there are some things I'd prefer not to share with you at this time."

"Like your family history?"

He shifted gear as the car approached a hairpin bend on the lakeshore road. "No. It's not my favorite subject, but if it's all that important to you, I'll tell you what there is to know."

"It's that important, Dominic. You're my baby's father."

"Okay." Steering skillfully through the curve, he shifted again into high gear. "My mother gave birth to me when she was twenty. My father, who was thirty-eight, was her college professor, had a Ph.D. in literature and fancied himself a poet. He believed in love, especially if it was free, but wasn't big on follow-through. When my mother told him she was pregnant, he suddenly remembered he was married and due for a year's sabbatical leave. He gave her a thousand dollars to buy an abortion if that's what she wanted, packed up his wife and personal possessions and was busy spouting iambic pentameters at some campus in Kentucky when I was born six months later in Vancouver."

He spoke lightly, as if what he had to say was of little consequence, but the set of his jaw and his grip on the steering wheel told Sophie that it was what he left unsaid that counted.

"Did your mother tell your father that she'd decided to go through with the pregnancy?"

"No. He'd already made it plain he wasn't interested in what she did."

"How sad."

"The only sad part," Dominic said, his words forged from steel, "is that my mother actually loved the jerk and continued to do so for the rest of her life. She died of acute cirrhosis when she was thirty-eight."

"Oh!" Sophie couldn't contain a small gasp of dismay as the implication of his disclosure struck home.

Without taking his eyes off the road, he nodded. "That's right, she was a drunk. A two-bottle-a-day woman by the time her liver gave out."

Sophie would have liked to touch his arm, to do something that would convey her sympathy. But he had walled himself off so thoroughly that there might as well have been a pane of glass separating her from him. So she said the conventional, hopelessly inadequate thing. "I'm very sorry, Dominic."

"Don't be. She was a lost, unhappy woman, abandoned by my father and disowned by her family. She didn't give a tinker's damn about her life. It just took her a long time to end it, that's all."

"But she had you. Surely that must have brought her some comfort?"

"I'm afraid not. Being saddled with a child and forced to support him by taking on whatever menial job she could find fell a long way short of postgraduate studies in Paris and love in the afternoon with my father."

"So you're not close to your grandparents?"

His laughter ricocheted around the interior of the car. "Grandparents?" he inquired mockingly. "Don't they belong to the same make-believe world as Santa Claus and tooth fairies?"

"But what about your father? Did he never change his mind and decide he wanted to get to know his son after all?"

"My *father* and I," Dominic said, referring to his other parent so scathingly that she flinched, "have spent the grand total of forty-five minutes in each other's company at the end of which time we parted in mutual relief. I went looking for him, convinced I could make him see the error of his having walked out on us, and he made it clear he harbored not a single regret for his decision. I was sixteen at the time, which is the only excuse I can offer for being such a bloody fool, but after, I vowed that no one would ever shove me aside again as if I was of no account. I'd be in control. And damn it, I have been."

"Do you have any half brothers or sisters?"

"No. Children, the good professor informed me, were a scourge not to be tolerated, and I can quite see how they would have cramped his style. Imagine trying to preserve the image of dashing lover if you have to cut short the big seduction to take your kid to football practice!"

"I cannot imagine anyone turning his back on his only child," Sophie said softly.

"Good. Then you should have no trouble understanding why I'm not about to stand back and let you raise our son or daughter alone. I intend to be a very immediate presence in my child's life. And one other thing you can count on, Sophie, is that I'm not cut from the same cloth as my old man. One woman at a time is quite enough for me."

There was no reason for the little flame of optimism that warmed her at that, but it flared up anyway.

He turned down the lane that led to her house. On the right, a pewter swath of moonlight dappled the surface of Jewel Lake.

"Will you let me come in for a minute?" he asked, drawing the car to a stop at her front door. "There's one thing we haven't discussed that needs to be taken care of right away."

In light of his revelation of past rejections, it seemed unfeeling to refuse. Once inside the house, he stalked uninvited through the main floor, ending up in the kitchen. There he paused for a moment, surveying its cramped dimensions, then pushed aside the curtain covering the window in the door and stared through the darkened panes to the garden outside. Puzzled, she trailed after him.

"How much land do you have here, Sophie?" he asked.

"Just over an acre."

"With how much lakefront?"

"About a hundred and fifty feet."

"And you hold clear title?"

"I have a mortgage, as I told you last night."

"Oh, that!" He snapped his fingers dismissively, as if the matter of thousands of dollars owed to the bank was small potatoes to a man of his means. "No, I'm talking about freehold title. You're not on leased land, are you?"

"No."

"Excellent. Given the state of this building..." He thumped the door frame, which set the glass to rattling alarmingly. "Hell, it's about ready to fall down on its own without any help from me."

"I'm not sure I'm following you, Dominic."

He waved an airy hand around the kitchen, embracing its old-fashioned cabinets and temperamental plumbing. "I'm going to knock down your house, Sophie, and build you something better."

"What if I don't want my house knocked down?" she said, less because of her attachment to the drafty old thing than because she resented the way he dismissed it.

It seemed to occur to him that he was pushing his luck a little in taking so much for granted. Bathing her in one of those rare and charming smiles normally reserved for other people, he asked, "Wouldn't you like something more convenient? Something with fewer stairs and higher ceilings?'' With both hands, he painted broad, sweeping strokes across an imaginary canvas. ''Think of a house with wide hallways and French doors that open onto patios that face the lake. Picture a breakfast nook flooded with morning sunshine, a formal dining room for parties. His-and-her en suite bathrooms with jetted tubs. Nanny's quarters next to a bright, airy nursery. Hardwood floors and marble countertops, modern appliances and light fixtures. Space to move without bumping into things.''

The dinosaur of a furnace chose that moment to clank into operation.

''And six-zone hot-water heating that neither makes a noise nor fills the air with the accumulated dust of the past fifty years,'' Dominic said, swooping in for the kill.

If he thought he could bulldoze her the way he planned to bulldoze her house, he was in for a big surprise. ''This house is good enough for me,'' she said, knowing it was a lie and that she'd give her eyeteeth for the kind of house he'd described.

''Well, it's not good enough for my baby—or my wife, come to that,'' he informed her. ''You're already concerned about the conclusions your parents will reach about our marriage when they find out you're pregnant, and I'm not about to add fuel to their speculation by allowing you to remain in a hovel like this.''

He would not *allow*? ''You—you have no right to belittle the way I live,'' she spluttered, incensed.

''Don't I have the right to want to give my child the best I can afford?''

Unaccountably depressed by his reply, she turned away and stroked an affectionate hand over the worn Formica counter. Granted, the house wasn't a palace, but she'd been happy here and she couldn't shake the feeling that, all its modern luxuries notwithstanding, the home he planned would be sadly lacking in that one commodity.

"You think money can buy anything you want, Dominic, don't you? You think, because you've got money and I haven't, that you can just barge into my life and take it over." She swung back to face him. "Well, I won't stand for it."

"In case you've forgotten, there's a line in the marriage ceremony that goes something like 'with all my worldly goods I thee endow'," he shot back. "And if there's one vow I can keep, it's that."

He was glaring at her, his eyes shooting green sparks of anger. His beautiful mobile mouth that, even without trying or really meaning to, could turn out kisses sweet enough to soften any woman's resistance was pressed into a hard, uncompromising line. And suddenly, Sophie knew she wanted more from him than just the promise of his worldly goods. She wanted things that had nothing to do with money, things that he wouldn't dream of giving to any other woman, that he would save for her alone.

She wanted to see him look at her across a room full of people, his eyes molten with desire—for her. Wanted his fists to uncurl now and close over her shoulders in persuasion. Wanted him to reach out in unadorned hunger and pull her so close that she could feel the proof of his arousal pressing against her, then sweep her into his arms and carry her upstairs to bed.

She had every reason in the world to despise him. He'd shown himself to be cold, bitter, judgmental, not to mention unnaturally controlled in the face of Barbara's death. Yet he made Sophie's heart flutter and stall and filled her wicked mind with images of his face hovering over hers, his mouth closing on hers, his body...

Dear heaven, she had the moral fiber of an alley cat in heat! Was this what the hormonal upheaval of pregnancy did for a woman—turn her into a raving nymphomaniac? She blinked and gave herself a mental shake. "I'm not for sale, Dominic."

Surprisingly, his shoulders slumped. "I never thought you were," he said tiredly, "and if that's the impression I've given you then I'm sorry."

So am I, she thought, *because the real problem here is that you and I have never been able to communicate except for one memorable time when, although we shared our bodies, we never bared our hearts or souls to each other.* "What I've already got is good enough for me," she said, the hollow untruth of her statement ringing in her ears.

Did he hear it, too? Or was it possible that he also regretted the dearth of emotional closeness between them? Was that what made him ask so gently that he verged on tenderness, "But wouldn't you like something better for the baby?"

Small wonder he was so successful in business if he always pinpointed his opponent's weak spot so accurately! "And if I do, where am I supposed to live while all these miracles occur?" she whispered, her resistance crumbling into dust.

"With me, naturally. I have a place downtown and it'll only be for a month or two. We'll be well settled in the new house before the baby arrives."

In a flash, her opposition resurfaced. "Did it ever occur to you that I might not be the type who believes in living with a man before marriage?"

The silent scorn with which he countered that feeble argument spoke for itself: *Where were your lofty moral principles the day you fell into bed with a stranger?*

And he was right. Her layers of deceit were building faster than even she could count. When had she slipped from attraction so covertly disguised that she could pretend it didn't really exist, to this contagious madness? When had he gone from shadowing her waking fantasies to possessing her nighttime dreams?

She couldn't bear the gnawing hunger ripping at her, the feeling that she'd lost control of her life and been tossed into an emotional whirlpool.

"Would you really feel more comfortable staying with your parents until after the wedding?" he asked, his voice as neutral as his expression.

And try to hide from their observant eyes her morning sickness and her heartsickness, and heaven only knew what else?

She shook her head. "No. They have only one bedroom in the apartment and a pull-out sofa in the den for overnight guests. We'd be falling all over one another."

"Then you don't have much choice. It's my place or a hotel, and if you think your father's suspicious now, wait until he discovers you're camping out in a rented room."

He'd won again, the way he always did, Sophie thought wearily.

"So that's where we're at," she said, blowing a strand of hair out of her eyes and grimacing at Elaine, who was helping her empty her kitchen cupboards into cardboard boxes. "The wheels have been set in motion and all of a sudden not only am I pregnant and engaged, I'm about to become homeless."

"Hardly that! You're moving into a pretty plush apartment with Dominic Winter, Palmerstown's most eligible bachelor." Elaine breathed his name on the same awestruck breath that other people mentioned sightings of Elvis.

"You're beginning to sound like a broken record, Elaine," Sophie said irritably. "Yes, with Dominic Winter, and it's all your fault. If you'd had the chicken pox when you were a child like the rest of us, instead of waiting until you were pushing thirty, Barbara Wexler would be alive today, probably married to him herself, and I'd feel less like a woman heading down a mountain in a car whose brakes have failed."

Not in the least perturbed by the implication that she'd brought about one woman's death and condemned another to life imprisonment, Elaine continued to go about her work, saying only, "Don't blame me if you've fallen in love out of your league. I didn't twist your arm and force you to leap into bed with the man the first chance you got! You managed that all on your own."

"Fall in love?" Sophie's voice rose to a near shriek. "Don't be ridiculous! How could any right-minded woman fall in love with a man who's arrogant and over-bearing and secretive—not to mention in mourning? He's giving me his name, but Barbara Wexler's the one who has his heart and she took it to the grave with her."

Elaine sat back on her heels, a smug grin inching over her face. "Deny it all you like, old friend, but the signs are unmistakable. You're definitely well on the way to falling in love with him."

"Elaine, I don't even *like* the man!"

"And I can quite understand why you don't. From everything you tell me, he's not a very nice person. So why don't you just call his bluff and invite him to take a hike? Why assume a lifetime punishment for one little sin?"

Sophie was spared having to answer by the sound of the front door opening and the clump of several pairs of heavy boots coming down the hall. "That'll be him," she whispered. "He said he'd stop by with a couple of his workmen to go over the demolition plan."

"You mean I get to meet him?" Elaine could barely contain her delight. "Oh, be still my heart!"

"Shut up and behave yourself," Sophie hissed. "Things are bad enough without your making them any worse. Do you realize we'll be living together after today and I don't even know his birthday?"

"Try asking him. I'm sure he'd be only too glad to tell you."

"Tell you what?" he inquired, appearing in the doorway. "What do you want to know, Sophie?"

"Nothing," she mumbled. "I don't believe you've met my friend, Elaine."

"Hi, nice to meet you." He grinned with that special other-people charm. "How's the packing going?"

"As well as can be expected," Sophie announced primly.

The grin faded and he made the kind of face a man might make if he bit unexpectedly into a lemon. "I see. Do you think you'll be finished fairly soon?"

"Probably," she said, aware of Elaine rocking with silent laughter at her side. "Why?"

"Because I've got the truck outside and a couple of my men to help move things. Once I'm done going over next week's work schedule with them, I thought we'd load up all your stuff and haul it away to storage for you."

"I'm quite capable of taking care of it myself, Dominic," Sophie said.

"No doubt. However, those cartons are pretty heavy and I don't want you lifting them," he told her flatly.

"We'll be ready to load up in about half an hour, so try to have everything ready to go by then, okay?"

Sophie glared after his retreating back. "See what I mean?" she said through clenched teeth as the door swung closed.

"Oh, yes," Elaine murmured dreamily. "I see very well. No wonder you're in over your head. Sophie, he's gorgeous! He can impregnate me *any* time!"

She wasn't serious, of course, but that didn't prevent a totally irrational flash of jealousy streaking through Sophie. "Hardly gorgeous!" she scoffed. "He's too tall and lanky."

"Sleek and muscular," Elaine insisted.

"Bossy," Sophie snapped.

Elaine subsided into giggles again. "Masterful."

"Coldly impersonal."

"Sexy."

"Hateful."

"Irresistible," Elaine said, sobering. "Admit it, Sophie. We've been friends too long for me to let you get away with fooling yourself a minute longer."

Sophie looked away, appalled as the truth of Elaine's words found its mark with the deadly accuracy of an arrow. For weeks there had been such a yearning inside her, such an ache. One born of wanting and dreaming. And loving. Long before those few days on St. Julian, she'd been fighting the attraction, telling herself it was wrong, immoral, unhealthy.

Like an oyster, she'd learned to live with the irritation and been so busy hoping it would simply go away that she hadn't noticed when it turned into a pearl. But now, with her soul stripped bare like her house, she saw it for what it really was.

Her agreeing to marry Dominic had nothing to do with his threats to claim custody of the baby, nothing to do with coercion. And everything to do with her wanting to be the woman he called his wife.

Once she'd admitted it, there was no going back, no more deluding or denying. Hopelessly, she recognized it for the kind of love that perhaps only a woman could know, something that transcended time or logic. It simply *was*, and like a pervasive and thoroughly hypnotic disease, it had taken control of her.

"Irresistible," she admitted, and burst into tears. "Elaine, what in the world am I going to do?"

CHAPTER SIX

"MARRY him, of course," Elaine said, as if that would solve all the problems.

"You seem to be forgetting he's still in love with Barbara," Sophie wailed. "How can I compete with a ghost?"

"Just because you can't make him forget her completely doesn't mean you can't have a good time trying. And you might even succeed, if you'd stop treating him as if he's something that crawled out from under the nearest rock."

"I don't!" Sophie protested, swabbing indignantly at her tears.

"If what I just witnessed is any indication, you certainly do. Good grief, Sophie, he's doing the best he can. He hasn't disowned the baby, he hasn't walked away from you, he's trying to do the decent thing. What more would you like?"

"For him to want me for who I am, not for what I'm bringing to his life and not because he feels responsible or guilty or anything like that."

"Then I suggest you change your tactics," Elaine replied, adding sagely, "Ever hear about catching more flies with honey than with vinegar?"

"If you think I'm going to grovel for his affections...!"

"Who said anything about groveling—although it strikes me that's exactly what you'd like *him* to do." Elaine heaved the last box onto the counter and dusted off her hands. "No, I think a bit of simple honesty might work wonders."

Sophie stared at her in horror. "I couldn't possibly tell him I'm in love with him!"

"Perhaps not, but you could stop behaving as if you find him repulsive."

"Lie down and play dead, you mean? Fat chance!"

Elaine sighed, pure exasperation written all over her face. "What's with you, Sophie? What's happened to the nice, reasonable woman I used to know, the one who always tried to see the other person's point of view?"

"She got buried under the mess her life's turned into."

"So start sorting it out, and do it soon, before the other half of this proposed partnership decides he hasn't struck quite the bargain he first thought. And while I'm dishing out home truths, here's another for you to chew on. Stop laying all the blame for this pregnancy on him. It took two, kiddo."

"I don't blame him."

"Not consciously, perhaps, but you're looking for someone to lambaste for what you call 'the mess her life's turned into', and he makes a convenient whipping boy."

Sophie bristled. "Well, I'm human, too, you know. And I don't like finding myself up to my ears in deceit—having to lie to my parents, to him, to myself. It's just not my style, Elaine."

"Then put an end to it. Stop letting yourself be manipulated by circumstances it's too late to change. He's willing to take a chance on marriage. Do your part to improve the odds in your favor."

"I hate you, Elaine Harrison," Sophie muttered, subsiding into a reluctant laugh. "Will you be my bridesmaid?"

"I'd already planned on it *and* on being the baby's godmother. They're two things you don't have any choice about," Elaine said, giving her a hug. "Now go and find that man of yours and invite him to take you out for dinner tonight. It might make going home to his place afterward a bit less strained if you both relax first over a meal and a bottle of good wine."

Things grew hectic shortly after that, what with a couple of the work crew loading all the furniture and boxes littering different rooms, and Elaine directing traffic, but Sophie took advantage of the activity to track down Dominic and try to make a fresh start.

She came across him in the dining room, where he was poring over blueprints spread across the table. "I'll get out of your way," he said politely when he noticed her hovering in the doorway, and started to roll up the sheets of paper.

He looked tired and more than a little discouraged. Enough to make Sophie wonder if she'd left it too late to adopt a less adversarial approach to their relationship. Daunted, she forced herself to stand beside him and rest a hand on his arm. "Are they the plans for the new house?"

He grew very still at the physical contact. "Yes."

She swallowed the nervousness clogging her throat. "May I see them?"

There was no reading the expression in his eyes. "If you wish, but there are still a few final details to be worked out."

"Still, I'd like to see, though I'll probably need you to explain things to me." It wasn't easy, offering the olive branch after all this time. His arm beneath her touch was iron hard, unresponsive. Dismayed, she tried to let her fingers slide unobtrusively to the sheaf of drawings on the table. "Is this how it'll look from the outside?"

His hand came down hard on hers, sandwiching it against the blueprint. "Drop the act, Sophie," he said stonily. "You're not so dense that you can't recognize the front elevation of a house when you see it, so what's this really all about?"

"Nothing," she said, coming as close to stammering as she had since she was about four. "I'm just...interested...."

"Really? Since when?"

Her throat ached with trepidation. He had never spoken to her so coldly, not even in the early days when he'd made no secret of his dislike of her. She swallowed and scraped together the dregs of her courage. "Since I came to see that you've been right all along and that we do need something bigger. My house really doesn't lend itself to raising a family."

"Is that all?"

"Well, I was thinking that..." She raised her chin and looked him in the eye, determined not to take the coward's way out. But his gaze, burning into her, shrivelled her confidence to ashes. "Oh, never mind, it doesn't matter."

"It matters, Sophie," he said, and this time there was a hint of velvet underlying the reserve in his voice. "What is it you were thinking?"

Was it possible that, with goodwill and effort, each might discover in the other a soul mate? Could they work together to put aside everything that had gone before? And even if they couldn't, didn't they have a moral obligation to try, for the baby's sake?

...a bit of simple honesty might work wonders, Elaine had said. *Do your part to improve the odds in your favor*.

Sophie blew out a long breath and jumped in with both feet. "I thought we might start over again, try to get along. Work together. Make the...best of...things."

His attention remained firmly fixed on her face, driving her to recklessness.

"I mean," she babbled, "I know this isn't what either of us planned, and if we had things to do over again we'd almost certainly do them differently. Not that I'm saying I don't want the baby or anything, you understand, but having it sprung on me—well, not sprung on me exactly. I mean, you weren't expecting it, either, and I'm not saying it was all your fault but...but... Damn it, Dominic, say something, even if it's only to tell me to shut up!"

"Shut up," he said.

She glared at him, stung. "Is that the best response you can come up with?"

"What else would you like me to do?"

She would never listen to Elaine's advice again. Never. "You could be gracious enough to accept my apology."

"Is that what you were offering, Sophie? An apology?"

No, she thought miserably, *I was offering a whole lot more than that, but you're not interested in accepting it*. That was dangerous thinking, though, especially with his continuing to pin her in a gaze that she feared saw far more than she intended to reveal.

Drawing what was left of her dignity around her like a shield, she said, "Yes. I know I've been a bit unreasonable of late. Put it down to hormones if you like, because I don't think I'm normally so hard to get along with. The thing is, I'm willing to make more effort if you are, particularly since we'll be living under the same roof as of tonight.''

''Very well, it's a deal. How would you like to seal it?''

''Seal it?''

He nodded and folded his arms across his chest. If his voice was a little less hostile, the expression in his green eyes remained unabashedly suspicious. ''That's right,'' he said. ''It's customary in business to sign a contract when a deal is closed. What had you in mind in this instance? Some sort of prenuptial agreement?''

He really must despise her if he figured she was the type to demand that sort of material security, she thought, stunned at how much it hurt to acknowledge the fact. ''No,'' she said, turning away before he caught the sparkle of tears in her eyes. ''Your word is good enough for me and I'm sorry if my behaviour of late gives you reason to doubt mine.''

She was almost at the door before he spoke again. ''How about something simple, then, like a handshake?''

How could she refuse without losing credibility? And how could she pretend a handshake would suffice when what she wanted was so much more?

She heard the floor creak as he moved, felt his presence at her back, and thought he must surely sense the desolation possessing her. ''If that's not enough, Sophie,'' he said, his voice rolling over her like syrup, ''all you have to do is say so.''

The tears were threatening to splash down her face and all she could think, foolish, vain creature that she was, was that she looked like hell when she cried. Her nose ran and her face contorted into what her twin, Paul, had once informed her reminded him of a pickled red cabbage. Pride would not allow her to present Dominic with such a sight. She was at enough of a disadvantage as it was.

"It's enough," she managed, struggling past the lump in her throat and, averting her face, thrust out her hand.

His fingers closed over hers and didn't let go. "Then look at me, Sophie," he commanded softly, drawing her round toward him, "and tell me why you're choking back the tears. Is it something I've done—or not done?"

"It's got to be the pregnancy," she said on a pathetic little sob. "I never cry as a rule, but lately I'm an emotional mess."

"How so?" he asked, his voice a murmuring caress.

She dashed the tears away. "I don't know! If I did, I'd do something about it. I hate these wild emotional outbursts."

She hated the aching need to be close to him, too—the vicious, ceaseless hungering that nothing but his touch, his kiss, could assuage. But she couldn't control it, so when he opened his arms to her, she flung herself into them with an abandon quite foreign to her normal nature.

It didn't matter, though. All that counted was that at last she was exactly where she wanted to be. She pressed her face against the soft flannel of his shirt and closed her eyes, drowning in the safe, masculine strength of him. He held her close, stroking his hands up and down her spine in long, sensuous sweeps and she thought that perhaps his heart started to drum just a little faster and his breath to emerge more raggedly.

She even went so far as to allow herself the luxury of believing that perhaps, one day, he might fall a little bit in love with her, too. Enough for her to dare say, "There's so much that still has to be arranged, so much we haven't yet talked about. I wondered if tonight—?"

Then the door opened and one of his workmen stuck his head into the room. "Call for you, boss," he announced, holding out a cellular telephone. "It's Mrs. Wexler. Thought I'd better let you know since you mentioned you were waiting to hear from her."

"Yes, thanks." Disengaging himself from Sophie, Dominic took the phone. "Hello, Gail, how are you?... No, of course I hadn't forgotten.... Oh, sure, six-thirty's fine.... Yes, looking forward to it...."

Sophie felt a chill where seconds earlier she'd absorbed warmth. Felt a mere yard stretch a mile of distance between her and Dominic. She saw the smile that turned up the corners of his mouth as he listened to Gail Wexler; heard the softening in his voice, the affection. And knew that nothing he'd ever offered her came even close to what he gave so freely to Barbara's mother.

This evening she was moving into his apartment. They would be sharing breakfast, the morning paper, even a bed if that was what she wanted. Their wedding might still be two weeks away, but to all intents and purposes they were starting their marriage today. And tonight, when she'd hoped they might bridge the awkwardness of the transition with a quiet dinner for two, she found he'd already made plans to spend the evening with his late fiancée's parents.

The message was clear. It would take a lot more than Sophie could offer to relegate Barbara to second place in his life.

As unobtrusively as possible, she edged toward the open door. When he noticed anyway and, without breaking the thread of his conversation with Mrs. Wexler, raised his hand and mouthed, "Hold on a minute," Sophie pretended she hadn't seen and kept on going.

Although the snow had gone from town, traces of it still remained under the trees bordering the paths of Heron Hill Provincial Park on the far shores of Jewel Lake. It was deserted that February afternoon, a bleak and lonely sort of place that echoed Sophie's mood.

Down near the beach, she found a picnic bench sheltered from the wind playing briskly over the waves. Wrapping her arms around her knees, she huddled inside her coat and stared across the water to Palmerstown's skyline squatting at the foot of the inland hills.

Dominic's penthouse apartment crowned one of those buildings just coming alight as day faded into dusk. She had seen its spacious rooms: the self-contained guest suite that was to be hers for the next several months, the streamlined kitchen, the comfortable living area with its deep leather couches, the dining room austerely furnished in smoked glass and teak.

Those things she'd need in the immediate future, her clothing and personal items, waited to be unpacked from the suitcases and neatly labeled boxes stacked at the foot of the bed. In separate, sturdier cartons were a few special pieces intended to make her feel more at home: her favorite painting, a couple of lamps, Paul and Jenny's wedding portrait.

Tomorrow her desk would be delivered, along with her houseplants. The key Dominic had given her a few days ago lay coldly in her palm. Everything she needed to take up residence was ready and waiting. Except her courage.

That was why she'd come out to this place of solitude: to try to drum up the fortitude to deal with the bald reality of her future. It wasn't the fact that Dominic had made other arrangements for an evening she'd wanted to spend with him that had driven her to find this windswept, barren spot more than sixty miles away from town; it was the dull certainty that he would repeat the pattern.

There would be many other evenings and days—and perhaps even nights—when she would find herself not a part of his plans. If she hadn't been so busy hiding from her real feelings, she might have seen that such an arrangement was probably part and parcel of every marriage of inconvenience and prepared herself for it.

A month ago, when self-deception had all been part of the game, she might have said it didn't matter if they went their separate ways much of the time. She might have argued it was better that way and that the less they saw of each other, the easier it would be on both of them. But then, a month ago she hadn't bargained on the jealousy and pain that came of unrequited love, any more than she had on finding herself its prisoner.

Only now, when it was much too late to change anything, did she discover that what bound her to Dominic was not the right he'd demanded to share fully in the upbringing of their baby, but the utter claim he'd staked on her heart.

What made matters worse was knowing that, even though nothing but empty rooms awaited her, she would eventually drive back over the winding road to Palmerstown, past the turnoff to her once-and-future home, and all the way along Lakeshore Drive to the elegant white condominium building that Dominic had built and owned. And she would do so not because he would be waiting to welcome her to his luxurious top-floor apartment, but because she could not live without him and would take whatever crumbs he tossed her way as long as she could be near him.

She would let herself in with her borrowed key, unpack her suitcases, arrange her clothes in the mirrored closet, bathe in the deep marble tub and climb into the wide, empty bed. When tomorrow came, she would smile to cover her heartache and pretend that she didn't care if he preferred to cling to the past by spending time with the Wexlers.

Instead, she would concentrate on the future and the baby. *Their* baby, hers and Dominic's. Because a baby was the one thing Barbara had not given to him.

A sudden gust of wind sent the skeletons of last year's leaves swirling around the picnic bench and drove the chill of late afternoon inside the folds of her coat. It was time to go.

About forty miles from the outskirts of Palmerstown, she stopped at a roadside inn for a meal. She had eaten nothing since breakfast, and although it was easy enough to ignore her own hunger pangs, she would do nothing to endanger her baby's health. Apart from any other consideration, the baby was her passport to a future with Dominic.

The penthouse was dim and quiet when she stepped through the front door. Beyond the foyer, the floor-to-ceiling windows that lined one wall of the living room glimmered with light from nearby buildings, enough for her to find her way to the hall that led to the bedroom wing.

She was perhaps halfway past the open archway leading to the living room when the entire place was flooded with sudden light. From the depths of a wing chair that matched the leather couches, a voice demanded rawly, "Do you know what time it is?"

Badly shaken, she spun around, shading her eyes against the glare. "Dominic, you scared me! I thought you weren't home."

He rose to his feet, lithe and lethal in the rage he made no effort to hide. "I asked you, do you know what the hell time it is?"

"Ah... about eight o'clock?" she managed over her thundering heart.

"Try closer to nine-thirty," he said, advancing on her with such deadly intent that she found herself backing away until, abruptly, she came up against the wall. "And what I want to know is where the f— have you been until now?"

"Dominic!" Shocked, she stared at him and saw a black-clad stranger, a man so close to not being in control that she almost cringed.

The breath hissed between his lips as he fought for composure. "I'm waiting, Sophie. Where were you?"

"Out," she said with a bravado that crumbled when she saw his fingers curl into fists. She swallowed and added hurriedly, "I drove out to Heron Hill Park."

"At this time of year?" he sneered, skepticism blazing in his eyes. "You can do better than that, Sophie."

She inched to the left, trying for a little distance between them. "Believe it or not as you choose, but that's where I was. I stopped for dinner the other side of Beaver Creek."

"I have been waiting for you to come home for the past two hours," he said, the menace in his tone only slightly contained.

"No, you haven't," she replied, too outraged by his lie to weigh the wisdom of attacking him in his present mood. "You dined with your erstwhile future in-laws, the Wexlers, so don't pretend you've been hanging around here waiting for me. I'm sure I was the last thing on your mind!"

Very briefly, he showed surprise at her outburst, although he hid it rather better than she had managed hers when he'd accosted her so suddenly. His shoulders stiffened beneath the black sweater, his brows drew together, his mouth assumed a grim line, and it occurred to her, in a flash of mental irrelevance, that he was all dark parallel bars of displeasure.

"The Wexlers returned today from a six-week cruise to the Orient—" he began in measured tones.

Her voice rang out, shrill with accusation, and not for the life of her could she silence it. "And you couldn't wait to rush over and welcome them home, could you? I understand perfectly, Dominic. You don't have to explain. Although it does strike me that all your talk about wanting to make a go of marriage with me amounts to a load of rubbish as long as your real allegiance lies with the parents of your late fiancée."

"For your information," he cut in, so icily that goose bumps prickled over her skin despite her heavy winter coat, "I spent precisely three-quarters of an hour with Barbara's parents and that only because I thought it fair that I be the one to tell them I was shortly getting married to you."

Dismay flooded through her. "Oh," she moaned, covering her face with both hands.

"They send you their very best wishes and their love. Unlike you, my dear Sophie, they are able to separate the past from the present."

"I'm so sorry! I'm afraid that once again I jumped to the wrong—"

"And then," he continued remorselessly, "I came back here, assuming I'd find you and intending to act on your suggestion this afternoon that we make a fresh start. I thought perhaps dinner at Le Coq D'Or might be in order. I did not know you had taken offense because we were interrupted by a phone call. I had, after all, indicated to you that our conversation was not finished, that there still were things we had to say to each other."

A spate of excuses bubbled up, but in the end all she could mutter again was, "I'm sorry," because, pitifully inadequate though they were, they were the only words to express her remorse.

"So am I." He sighed and turned away, leaving her blind with regret.

She wished for so many things. That she could go back to that moment just before she'd fallen in love with him—that time of utter self-containment. That just once he'd look at her with desire smoking in his eyes and let his smile warm her...secret, knowing.

To her shame, that familiar flush of jealousy attacked again at the thought that Barbara, for however short a time, had known Dominic's love and the outpouring of his passion. It lessened the tragedy of her death somehow, and left Sophie numb with horror at her own mean-spirited, unfeeling envy.

Dominic swung back toward her. "We seem to spend a great deal of time apologizing to one another, Sophie, and yet somehow there's never a sense of real regret. We don't change, we don't make things better. You continue to resent me, blame me—"

Why couldn't she tell him that wasn't true, instead of aiming the accusation back at him and insisting, "No, it's the other way around. *You* feel trapped, and if you could, you'd find a way to get free of me. I know it, here—" she clutched a fistful of coat in front of her heart "—and that's why I thought you'd chosen to spend the evening with people you associate with..." She wanted to speak Barbara's name, to spit it out like the bad taste it was in her mouth, but she didn't. She'd done enough already, leaping to false conclusions and hurling accusations. "...happier times," she finished lamely.

He strode to the bar at the far end of the living room and poured a dollop of whiskey into a heavy crystal glass. "I asked you once before not to try to second-guess how I feel or what I'm thinking. I have many faults, as a lot of people in this town will be only too glad to tell you, but I like to think that moral dishonesty of the kind you describe is not among them, so let me spell it out for you one last time. Barbara is dead and you are not. *You*, not she, will be my wife. As such, you will never have cause to question my loyalty."

He made her feel small and unworthy and so lacking in generosity that she wanted to curl up and die. If ever there was a time to call forth that simple honesty Elaine had prescribed, it was now. But not with words. All words had ever done was create barriers between the two of them.

Swirling the whiskey in his glass, he paced restlessly back and forth in front of the fireplace. She hovered just within the room's entrance, despair a leaden weight rooting her to the spot.

It wasn't the silence stretching unbroken between them that daunted her; it was the invisible shield of aloofness separating her from him. Either she broke through it now or she looked into a future bereft of any sort of closeness between them.

Whoever had decreed that the first step was always the hardest forgot to add that it went beyond difficult to sheer torture. The way was not straight and easy but a tightrope of uncertainty swinging without benefit of safety net above a chasm of fear.

Sophie lifted one foot, and then the other. Prayed for endurance and fortitude. Fought the temptation to turn tail and run to the safety of her solitary room. If only he'd reach out and draw her past the obstacles and into the haven of his arms! If only she could read the thoughts inside his dark, handsome head, see beyond the unsmiling dispassion that carved his beautiful face!

His gaze raked over her, deep and mysterious as a forest pool. She paused, hoping for some sign from him—even rejection—because nothing could be worse than this, with her teetering midway between heaven and hell.

He heaved a great sigh and, as though he couldn't bear the sight of her, swung away to face the mantelpiece.

His dismissal broke her heart. Blinded by tears, she stumbled toward him and pressed her cheek against the unyielding line of his spine. "Dominic!" she begged, naked yearning tearing at her voice, and for once it was the right thing to say.

She heard the groan deep in his throat, the crack of Baccarat on marble as he slammed down his glass on the mantelpiece and swung toward her. A string of words escaped him, four-lettered every one and laced with frustration.

They sang in her ears like music and her heart lifted just a little. A man didn't curse like that, did he, unless something...someone had slipped past his guard and found the sweet, vulnerable soul he kept so well protected?

She felt his hands in her hair, his lips at her temples, at her tear-streaked eyes. And then, at last, at her mouth, demanding, asking and finally begging.

She wrapped her arms around his waist and clung to him. At his urging, she sank with him to the carpet. She stretched beside him and, without saying another word, told him in a thousand different ways that this was what she wanted: to be here, with him, and that if he wanted her, all he had to do was take her.

He wanted her. Too badly to try to hide it. His kisses trailed fire down her throat. He wreaked havoc with her clothing, shoving aside her coat, pulling her free of its confinement and flinging it behind him. She heard buttons wrench free from the fabric securing them; felt sudden coolness on her skin as her blouse fell away, swiftly followed by the warmth of his mouth at her breast.

Her skirt rode to her hips. His palm stroked up her calf, swept along her thighs, nudged them apart. She knew the instant he encroached beyond the frail barrier of her panties to reduce her to searing, flooding delirium, but had no idea when audacity guided her to exact a similar revenge and take the silken weight and vigor of him in her hands.

Somewhere from the back roads of memory, she recalled that first time on St. Julian and the hurried, furtive coupling that had taken place. Even then, there had been magic of a kind. But this time it was intensified a thousand times because, whereas then they had not acknowledged each other except in the most primal way, this time the connection was more complete, a physical union cemented by shared hope for the future. Along with their clothes, so many layers of fear and misunderstanding melted away.

"I had no idea you had changed so much," he muttered hoarsely, his eyes devouring the lush contours conferred on her by pregnancy. "Do you know how beautiful I find you?"

He made her heart sing. She—slight, unremarkable Sophie Casson—felt voluptuous. Desirable.

A short time later, when she pressed herself to him, reveling in the close tangling of his limbs with hers and the proud thrust of his erection at the juncture of her thighs, he muttered, "I want you so badly, Sophie, I'm afraid. What if I hurt you or the baby?"

And she felt cherished, treasured.

"You won't," she whispered, opening herself to him. "Hurry, Dominic, please. I need you. Let me feel you inside me."

Loving him with her eyes, her hands, her soul, she wrapped her legs around his waist, tilted up her hips and captured him. She saw the sweat break out on his forehead, felt his tension as he fought to exercise restraint. And felt whole for the first time in months when he lost the battle and buried himself deep within her.

She had known desire before. At least, she thought she had. But it was only then, in Dominic's arms, with the fires of passion raging between them and creating such turmoil in her blood, that she realized she'd known nothing.

Less than nothing. Because this was passion that went beyond mortal cognizance to approach the sublime. He could take whatever he wanted of her and she would give until she had nothing left to give. And then she would give some more.

"Wow!" he breathed when the clenching shudders subsided. Lifting his head, he grinned at her, a marvelous shining joy curving his mouth. "Would you like to do that again some time?"

Simple truth. "Yes," she said. "Often."

"Here?" The smile crept past the thick sweep of his lashes to his eyes. "I can light the fire to make it more romantic."

"I'd miss you," she said.

"You wouldn't have time. All I need to do is reach up and press the switch that turns on the gas." He lifted himself and leaned on one elbow. "Or we could behave like the decorously married couple we'll soon be and retire to the bedroom.''

"Yours?'' she inquired pertly, raking a fingernail through the dusting of dark hair on his chest. "Or mine?''

He sobered and cupped her face in his palm. "How about ours?''

He told her he loved her all night long, if not with words then in the ardor with which he possessed her more than once as the hours slid by, and in the way he held her during the times in between.

When she awoke, he was beside her still, pushing the hair away from her face and kissing her. He promised her breakfast in bed but made love to her instead. And she couldn't keep the feelings to herself. She had to try to seal them with words.

"I wish it could always be like this, Dominic,'' she breathed, rippling around him as ecstasy took hold.

"Just keep this moment,'' he panted, fighting to stave off completion. "Hold it to you and remember it tomorrow, next year—whenever you feel unsure.''

She held him close and rode with him, too consumed with the fire to say what she really wanted to say, which was that she had loved him for a long time and would do so for the rest of her life.

There would be time enough for that. There might even be a time when he would say the same thing to her.

"I'm not going into the office today,'' he told her after breakfast. "I've got a load of paperwork to wade through but I can do it here. That way I'm handy if you need help with any of those boxes.''

"It's mostly clothes,'' she said, suddenly unsure of herself again. Did he expect her to share his room now, or would that be an occasional thing only? Deeming it wiser not to push too hard, too soon, she continued, "I guess I'll get started hanging them in the guest room."

He combed his fingers through his hair and laughed. "That's probably best. My closet's a mess. You'll have to take me in hand and cure me of my bachelor ways when we move into the house."

For the first time, she dared to believe they could break free of the past. The future shone full of bright optimism, with no premonition of disaster to darken it.

Humming to herself, she lifted lingerie from her open suitcase and folded it neatly in the paper-lined drawers of the triple dresser running along one wall of the guest room. The ringing of the doorbell didn't rouse her to alarm; it didn't even interrupt her singing. There was nothing in the world that could spoil her happiness.

She was marginally conscious of Dominic crossing the marble-tiled foyer to the front door and of the nano-second of silence that followed. And still that famed intuition with which all women were supposedly blessed failed to alert her. She was blithely, utterly caught up in her fantasy of happily-ever-after, which perhaps accounted for her taking so long to register the reality of what happened next.

The laugh penetrated first, rippling through the penthouse like quicksilver, followed almost immediately by the unforgettable voice. "No, Dom darling, you're not seeing a ghost! It's me, Barbara! I'm alive after all!"

The words hit Sophie like a body blow. Recoiling, she clutched the edge of the dresser. But the carnage had only just begun.

Not content with the pain it had already inflicted, the lilting, confident voice dealt the ultimate coup de grace to Sophie's pitiful little dreams. "And guess what, darling. Miracle of miracles, I'm pregnant! We're going to have a baby, Dom! Isn't it wonderful?"

CHAPTER SEVEN

PAUL and Jenny were living in Bath, in England's West Country. Not far away was Wells, ancient and imperturbable, a place blessed with a timeless serenity that might, in time, heal her. Sophie knew the minute she walked in the shadow of its cathedral that she'd found a haven.

"But why not stay with us?" Jenny asked that night over dinner. "There's enough room here and we won't intrude on your privacy."

Not intentionally, perhaps, but they knew her whole pathetic story, and, well-meaning though Jenny was, Sophie couldn't take the inevitable flood of sympathy, the constant reminders of Dominic and the fact that she was pregnant and alone. As if she was likely to forget! "No," she said, "but I love you for asking."

"But you don't know anyone in Wells and you shouldn't be by yourself right now."

"I *need* to be by myself, Jenny."

"It isn't right!" Jenny's brown eyes filled with sympathetic tears. "You should be with the father of your child. I hope the rat fries for the hell he's putting you through!"

"He didn't ask me to leave," Sophie pointed out. "It was my decision to put distance between us by catching the first flight over here."

Jenny threw up her hands in frustration and turned to Paul. "Can't you talk her out of this? She doesn't

121

know a soul in Wells. What if she needs us? What if she becomes ill, or has an accident? Who'll let us know?''

Paul leaned back in his tufted leather chair, the smile he directed at Sophie telling her she didn't have to explain. He understood, just as he always had; neither time nor distance had weakened the bond between them. "Twin telepathy", Jenny had once called it. "We're a phone call away. Leave it, honey," he told his wife, then asked Sophie, "You want to borrow our car to go house hunting?"

"I don't think so, thanks. Driving on the left takes a bit of getting used to, especially on these narrow country roads. I'll take the bus into Wells in the morning and let the estate agent who's showing me properties be the chauffeur."

Two mornings later, Sophie signed a short-term lease on a tiny furnished house fronted by a flagstone courtyard. At the back, enclosed by a stone wall, was a long, narrow garden, a secluded, tranquil place that trapped the gentle warmth of spring and promised refuge from the brisk winds of autumn. Yew trees grew along the bottom along with a willow, and there was a sheltered sunny spot outside the paned glass doors of the living room.

If she decided to extend her stay until after the baby was born, he'd sleep there, safe in his sleek English baby carriage, and awake to the sound of cathedral bells. He would grow up happy and healthy, with rosy cheeks and chubby little fists. He would smile when he saw his mother's face, and even though he wouldn't understand the words, she would read and sing to him and he would never guess the heartache surrounding his conception and birth.

Her determination to bring those things to her baby's life made Sophie's own unhappiness a little more bearable. Most of the time. Except for those nights when she awoke and felt her child stir within her, as though he knew that it was then, with the moonlight shining through the tiny paned windows of the bedroom, that the misery crept past her guard.

That last scene in the penthouse would flash to life, each detail as sharp and shocking as ever. She would see again Barbara launching herself into Dominic's arms—and of them closing securely around her. She would see Dominic's shell-shocked expression, the sudden widening of his eyes when he noticed Sophie watching from the end of the hall and the swift, unmistakable jerk of his head ordering her back into the bedroom, out of sight.

How long had she huddled like a refugee on the clothes-strewn bed, hearing muffled voices, Barbara's peal of laughter? How long after the front door closed again before she realized she was alone in the penthouse, both out of sight and out of mind?

It hadn't taken Sophie long to cram her things back into the suitcases, to scribble the note that gave away nothing of her misery or rage and expressed only the very rational opinion that, from the beginning, she and Dominic had rushed things. "I need time to come to terms with everything that's happened, even if you don't," she'd finished, "so please accept my decision to spend the next few weeks alone."

She had done the right thing, of course, but that didn't lessen the sadness. She would turn on her side on the thick feather mattress in her little English house and watch winter ease toward spring. Outside, the stark branches of a plum tree gradually grew fat with buds ready to burst into blossom. At the bottom of the garden, the willow turned green almost overnight.

The loneliness was a wound that never healed, the wanting—the sight, the scent, the touch of him—always aching even in sleep. But waking was the worst. Knowing the memory of him was a little more faded by the passing of another day, his loving, such as it had been, that much more removed.

She wrote to her parents and told them that things hadn't worked out with Dominic but that she was well and would come home in a month or two. She did not tell them about the baby because they would have been frantic with worry. And just in case Dominic felt obliged to try to track her down, she gave them Paul's address because she knew she could trust him to keep her whereabouts secret.

She became friendly with her next-door neighbor, Violet Barclay, a spry little widow of seventy. When Violet found out that Sophie was expecting a baby in September, she started to make a layette of exquisite hand-sewn garments with smocked yokes and embroidered hems.

The bonds of affection between the two women grew quickly, perhaps because they were both alone. On what should have been her wedding day, Sophie confided the whole story of her relationship with Dominic. It was such a relief to be able to talk openly about it to someone of Violet's objectivity and wisdom.

"You will survive, lass," she promised Sophie. "We women always survive, no matter how crushing the tragedies or disappointments imposed upon us. A part of this man will always be with you in the shape of his son or daughter. Look to that and the future you will make for your child."

With the onset of warmer weather in April, Sophie bought a little car and ventured farther afield, visiting such legendary places as Winchester and Cheddar Gorge and Stonehenge. Other days, she discovered tiny market towns with quaint names like Shepton Mallet and Yeovil.

Of them all, though, her favorite spot was Glastonbury. She found a sort of enchantment in the shade of its ancient ruins that countered that dreadful sense of loss brought on as the days since she'd left Dominic became weeks.

"It nourishes me somehow," she told Violet, "as if everything that happens to us here is part of some greater cosmic plan. I'm not explaining it very well, I guess, but I come away with a sense of—" she spread her hands, palms raised upward "—destiny at work."

Violet nodded. "It renews your soul and gives you the strength to go on," she said. "I understand perfectly."

Slowly, the hurting places inside began to heal a little, giving Sophie the stamina to accept the reality of her situation. If proof that she had never amounted to anything other than a stand-in for the real thing was what she wanted, the fact that almost eight weeks had passed and Dominic hadn't come looking for her was testimony enough. Even her baby, which he'd sworn he'd never abandon, had been relegated to a bit part once he'd learned he'd fathered a child with his true love. By now, he and Barbara were probably married.

"But we'll manage without him," Sophie told the baby. "We'll never be really alone. We'll always have each other and someday soon we'll go home again and you'll get to know the rest of your family. It'll be enough, I promise."

Dominic was tired of being thwarted, first by the parents, then the brother. Discovering that Sophie wasn't home when he finally tracked her down to the address he'd weaseled out of her sister-in-law was the last straw.

"You are disturbing the peace, young man," a refined English voice informed him. "Miss Casson is away for the day and I take great exception to your banging on her door like that. It will not bring her home any sooner."

He turned to find himself impaled by the stern gaze of a venerable old woman, who either stood about seven feet tall in her stockinged feet or else was perched on a stepladder on the other side of the wall from Sophie's garden. "Sorry," he said brusquely. "Do you know when she's expected back?"

Disapproving blue eyes peered over the rims of wire-framed glasses. "And if I do?"

Realizing belligerence would do nothing to advance his cause, Dominic adopted a more mannerly approach. "Pardon me, ma'am. I don't mean to be rude, but I've traveled a long way and I'm rather anxious to see her."

"You are the father of her child," the woman determined, eyeing him as if he was something scraped from the bottom of her shoe. "The man who, it appears, would like to have his cake and eat it, too. Am I not right?"

Taken aback, Dominic stared at her and wondered what the hell Sophie had said about him to instill such a bad impression on the old biddy. It wasn't often that he found himself at a loss for words, nor did he care for the experience. "Well, I'm not sure what you mean about the cake, but yes, I'm the father of her child," he finally managed.

The woman disappeared so suddenly that he half feared she'd fallen from her perch. A minute later, however, she reappeared in the gateway to Sophie's courtyard, all her five-foot-two-inch frame apparently intact.

"It's taken you long enough to get here," she scolded.

"It's taken me long enough to find out where she's been hiding."

"Well, now that you have, what are you going to do about her?"

He'd watched television sitcoms from Britain that featured people like this woman and had found them hilarious. In the flesh, though, such individuals weren't quite so funny. "With all due respect, ma'am, that's hardly any of your business."

"Then neither are Miss Casson's whereabouts any of yours," the old dame retorted, and marched back the way she'd come.

Grinding his teeth in frustration, Dominic steeled himself to patience. He'd waited this long to have things out with Sophie; he could wait a few hours more. One thing he did know: he wasn't about to be run off by her self-appointed watchdog next door.

Stretching out on the sun-warmed stone bench under the window next to her front door, he shaded his eyes with an up-flung arm and settled in for the duration. She'd decided that running away was the solution to their problems and had asked him not to come after her, but he was not by nature a patient man and he'd played along with her vanishing act for long enough.

The sun had disappeared behind the trees, leaving the garden full of purple shadows, when the creak of the iron gate leading to her courtyard alerted him to her homecoming. Lowering his arm, he turned his head so that he could watch her as she made her way along the flagstone path to the front door.

She did not notice him, and he seized the small advantage to study her. She wasn't glamorous like Barbara, not exotic. But she was lovely in a classical sense, a delicate molding of bone caressed by skin of exquisite texture and fragility. A sun goddess, all light and sunshine, where Barbara had been storm and gales.

And yet, she'd changed. Most obviously, she'd let her hair grow longer and wore it caught in a band at her nape. Then, halfway to the house, she reached up to pick a few flowers from the creeper hanging over the wall, and he noticed the swell of her abdomen beneath the loose sweater, the fullness of her breasts. Intellectually, he'd known that by now the physical evidence of her pregnancy would be fully apparent, but he hadn't expected the emotional realization to pack quite such a wallop.

Still unaware of her audience, she pressed a hand to her ribs, let it trail unselfconsciously over one breast to her throat, then ran a finger inside the cowl collar of her sweater and flicked free the tendrils of hair caught there. Dominic stared, captivated by the insidious seduction of her womanliness, its separate parts made all the more irresistible by her utter unawareness of the impact of the whole.

Just looking at her made him ache. He wanted nothing more than to limn the sweet dimensions of her in his two hands, to taste her mouth, inhale the scent of her hair, test the fragility of her pale and lovely skin.

He had thought himself braced to deal with any eventuality when he saw her again, had been prepared to use whatever means presented themselves to bend her to his will and bring her back to him. He had thought he'd be the one in control, that his surprise appearance would afford him the advantage. But he had not counted on the aroused stirring of his flesh or the tide of pure hunger that swept over him at the sight of her, and he did not like the way it undermined his purpose.

Discomfited, he swung his feet to the ground.

Aware of movement to her right, Sophie swung around in time to see a figure unfolding from the bench beneath the window box outside her living room. Even in the dusk of early evening, she recognized him. There were conceivably several hundred thousand men in the world possessed of a similar long-legged, lean-hipped, masculine grace, but only one who could make her heart sprint so unevenly that she felt as if the earth was falling away beneath her feet, taking with it every last particle of her hard-won peace and acceptance.

Dominic picked up his jacket, which he'd used as a pillow, and looping it over his thumb, slung it over his shoulder. "So," he drawled in the same honey-rich voice that had haunted her dreams, "you're finally home. I was beginning to think I was going to have to sleep out here."

As a lover's greeting, it fell distinctly short of romantic. Dark, provocative tone notwithstanding, he sounded peeved rather than relieved. That alone should have been enough to send up red-alert flags and remind Sophie that, with him, disenchantment always followed brief euphoria.

To her dismay, however, the old molten hunger surged up within her, all the more ravaging for its hiatus. The urge to run to him, to know just one more time the feel of his arms around her, the beat of his heart beneath her cheek, tore at her.

Forcibly restraining herself from any such action, she asked frigidly, "What do you want, Dominic?"

"Isn't it obvious?"

"If it were, I wouldn't have asked."

He swore long and colorfully.

When he stopped to draw breath, she said with a marvelous facsimile of composure, "How charming! You've obviously lost none of your skill at profanity since the last occasion I elected to distance myself from you when, as I recall, you were equally vulgar."

"Perhaps," he replied, thunderheads roiling through his voice, "because then, as now, you saw fit to try my patience beyond human endurance. This disappearing act you're so fond of pulling when you decide things aren't going quite the way you think they should is wearing thin, Sophie, particularly when there's no reason for it."

If he'd hoped to prick the fragile balloon of her self-control, he'd chosen the right way to go about it. "The way I see it, I had reasons to spare when Barbara Wexler came waltzing in your front door, crowing about carrying your baby," Sophie exploded. "With your prodigious capabilities, you could start your own sperm bank!"

After a moment's stunned silence, he burst out laughing, great hooting guffaws that had him doubled over. Sophie wanted very badly to scratch out his eyes, to kick him where it would do the most damage. But he'd made her feel foolish enough already; she wouldn't allow him to goad her into diminishing herself further.

"I'm so glad I've afforded you a little entertainment," she said, marching past him and thrusting open the front door. "I would hate to think you'd come all this way for nothing."

A gentleman would have taken the hint and left, but all the trappings to the contrary, Dominic Winter clearly was no gentleman. Before she could slam the door closed in his face, he'd shouldered his way into her tiny living room. "I came all this way to bring you home, Sophie," he declared, "and I have no intention of leaving without you."

"Then you really have wasted your time because I have no intention of going anywhere with you. I like it here. I am happy here. And I intend to stay here for as long as it pleases me."

He rolled his shoulders in a shrug and lowered his lashes to a sultry half-mast. "Hope you've got room enough in the bed for me, then," he purred.

Tamping down the unconscionable flash of delight that remark produced, Sophie snapped, "Stop playing games, Dominic! I'm serious."

His amusement vanished. "For once we're on the same plane, then, because I'm serious, too. We were supposed to be married over a month ago and instead what do you do? Sneak off the minute my back's turned and leave behind a two-line note that more or less tells me to kiss off and have a nice life."

Baffled, she stared at him. If she didn't know better, she'd almost be persuaded that he'd missed her. "I thought you'd be grateful I'd gone so quietly without making a fuss. After all, we both know I have no place in your life now that Barbara's back."

Shaking his head from side to side and rolling his eyes, he expelled a long, frustrated breath. "You're turning out to be one pack of trouble with your propensity for jumping to wrong conclusions, do you know that? You had no reason to run off, no reason at all."

She had thought herself resigned to losing him, had mapped out a future that, of necessity, didn't include him. Yet, at his words, a tiny flame of hope flickered to life. Doing her best to snuff it out before it brought her more pain than she could possibly bear, she affected a nonchalance she was far from feeling and said, "Well, it beat being asked to leave. Or did you expect me to sit quietly in my room and wait to be formally dismissed?" She laughed, a ragged, miserable effort that proved nothing except that her control was teetering on the brink of annihilation. "Sorry, Dominic, that's just not my style!"

"Are you so certain that's how things would have turned out, Sophie?"

"Oh, yes," she sighed, sudden weariness swamping her. "Just as I'm certain the only reason you're here now is to tell me that since you've got your hands full with Barbara and the baby she's expecting, I can come out of hiding and do what I wanted from the first without fear of interference from you."

"And what is it that you wanted?" he inquired softly.

"To be free to bring up my child without having to sell my soul first."

"I see. Well, if by that you think I'm about to simply turn my back—"

"Oh, I'm sure you'll try to sweeten rejection by offering to compensate the understudy."

"You're pushing your luck, Sophie," he warned, his tone soft and dangerous.

"Really?" Ignoring the inner voice of caution, she stared him in the eye and plowed on rashly, "Are you or are you not the man who once pointed out to me that money could buy anything? And what's a little payoff between . . . ?"

"Friends?" he suggested when she floundered to a halt. "Enemies?" He moved closer, trapping her between the fireplace and the overstuffed armchair next to it. "Or were you thinking more along the lines of 'lovers'?"

"You and Barbara were lovers," she said, wincing at the pain of the admission. "You never really wanted me."

She'd touched a nerve, no doubt about it. Anger tinted his eyes, sharpening their sultry jade to emerald fire, and for a brief instant she thought he might shake her. "Then what in the blue blazes did you think I had in mind when I asked you to marry me?" he roared, looming over her and dwarfing the room with his sheer presence.

The effort of pretending she didn't care a rap about him, when just seeing him again was tearing her apart, defeated her. If the only way she could be rid of him was to tell him the truth, then so be it.

"You didn't ask me," she said dully. "You suggested it was the right and logical thing to do, which led me to understand that your principles were involved but not your heart. And I wanted your heart. All of it. After all, I gave you mine."

The thundering silence of his response to that insane disclosure seemed to last a small eternity and was so much worse than anything else he could have offered. Disbelief, amusement, scorn—those she could have defined and dealt with, but not his tacit agreement that, indeed, he had never pledged himself to her for any but the most expedient of reasons.

Abruptly, she slipped past him. "Excuse me, please," she muttered, tossing the words over her shoulder as she disappeared into the sanctuary of her kitchen. "I left a casserole in the oven and I think I smell it burning."

He did not at first follow her, for which she was grateful. If he had a single sensitive bone in his body, he'd leave while her back was turned and spare them

both the embarrassment of trying to gloss over her un-
forgivable lapse.

Wrenching open the oven door, she hauled out the
casserole and discovered she hadn't told a complete lie
in order to escape him. The beef ribs she'd put in to
bake that morning badly needed basting if they were to
be edible. Yet all the time that she busied herself with
the task, her attention remained focused on the man she
could hear wandering around her living room, and she
knew to the second when he came to lean in the kitchen
doorway and watch her at work.

Suddenly clumsy, she burned herself on the oven-
proof dish. "Damn," she muttered, snatching back her
hand and sucking at the painful spot on her thumb.

He was beside her in a flash. "That's not going to do
much good." He reached over her shoulder to the sink
and turned on the cold water. "Hold your hand under
here instead. It'll reduce the burning."

But only in her thumb, she thought, and that was the
least disturbing thing that ailed her. The fire in her cheeks
and that other, more subtle heat that had flickered into
life at his touch flared with renewed savagery. The kitchen
was small enough at the best of times, but with him at
her back, it verged on the claustrophobic.

"I can manage," she insisted, and attempted to fend
him off with a backward thrust of her elbow.

But he was as solidly immovable as the proverbial
mountain. Holding her hand firmly under the stream of
water, he brought his mouth close to her ear and said
softly, "Did you really give me your heart, Sophie?"

"I suppose so—temporarily. But I soon realized I'd
made a dreadful mistake, so I took it back again."

He turned off the water and reached for the towel
hanging from a hook on the wall. Turning her around,

he very carefully dried her hand, then tipped up her chin so that she had no choice but to meet his gaze. "Are you sure?" he asked.

Quickly, before he saw in them the pain she couldn't hide, she closed her eyes. "Please, Dominic," she begged, her defenses crumbling into ruins, "don't do this. Please, say what you came to say and then just go. I really am very tired and don't think I can take much more today."

She felt his fingertips at her jaw, tracing its length from her earlobe to her lower lip. "And tomorrow, and the day after, and the day after that? What about them, Sophie? What about the future you and I had planned?"

"It died," she said dully, the tears seeping between her lashes, "the day Barbara showed up alive. And if you don't want to spell it all out for me because you think it's too cruel, then I'll say it for you. I was only ever second best and you had no reason to settle for that when the real love of your life came back. So go home, Dominic. Go back to your wife and leave me alone."

He caught the tears and swept them aside with the ball of his thumb. "Listen to me, you blind, willful creature," he commanded softly. "Barbara is not my wife, nor will she ever be. She and I are finished. We have been finished for quite some time."

They should have been the most reassuring words in the world. A month ago, a week even, Sophie would have sold her soul to hear them, yet now that they were hers to treasure, she looked for the conditions attached, the ones that would dash her hopes to pieces and send her spiraling back into the darkness from which she'd only recently begun to emerge.

"Because you thought she was dead," she said. "Now that you know she's alive, though—"

"It makes no difference, Sophie. Even if she was the same woman I once asked to marry me, I'm not the same man."

"But you loved her."

"I thought I did. I realize now I was mistaken."

Of all the questions to which she sought answers, the only one she ached to ask at that moment was, *Why*? *Because you love me*? But she was teetering again on that emotional tightrope, with despair on the one side waiting to engulf her, and she dared not take the chance of falling the wrong way. "And how does Barbara—?"

With fatal tenderness, he cupped her face in his two hands and pressed his thumbs to her mouth, sealing it closed. "Tomorrow, sweet Sophie, I'll explain everything," he whispered fiercely. "But for tonight, will you please just trust me enough to believe that I will never again allow anything or anyone to come between us? I flew halfway around the world and badgered your family into telling me where to find you because what I most want to do is set things right between us. And I'd like to begin with this."

His thumbs slid away to make room for his mouth. Threading his fingers through her hair and imprisoning her head so that she couldn't turn aside, he kissed one corner of her mouth and then the other. He kissed her eyelids and her nose, and then came back to her mouth. He drew his tongue in a sweet, damp line over her lower lip, banishing all the long, empty hours of missing him.

Yet it was her fault, not his, that things quickly escalated to a raging wildfire. He didn't push for more than she was prepared to give; he showed her every way he knew how that he was content to savor each delicious second without rushing ahead to the next. But his touch triggered an explosion within her that decimated every instinct for self-preservation she'd ever harbored.

She melted against him, ignoring the reasons for their estrangement, past caring that the higher she flew toward paradise, the harder she'd fall if it eluded her. Yes, she'd been hurt, and angry, and disappointed, but that was yesterday and this...oh, this was now, and closer to heaven than she'd ever thought to find herself again!

She closed her eyes, luxuriating in the scent and warmth of him. Her mouth softened in tacit connivance, letting him know that she would give anything and everything he chose to ask of her.

Shamelessly, she angled against him, wedging her thigh between both of his, there where he was most vulnerable to seduction. Her hands tugged his shirt free of his trousers and burrowed beneath it to search out the smooth planes of his back.

The consequences were instantaneous and irrevocable. A tremor shook him as though a thousand demons battered at him, urging him simply to take her there and then, between stove and sink, and to hell with the finer points of protocol.

He deepened the kiss, clouding her mind to any other perception but the certain knowledge that she needed him, hard and imperative inside her, claiming her body just as he'd long ago claimed her soul.

"What about the casserole?" he murmured on a strangled breath.

"To hell with the casserole," she said, then felt her heart spill over with all the love she'd tried so hard to contain when, with unwavering purpose, he swept her up in his arms and swung toward the narrow staircase opposite the front door.

Apart from a small bathroom, the upper story of the house consisted of only one room with a windowed alcove at the far end that she'd planned to turn into a nursery, and a floor that sloped unevenly toward the east.

The bed, an ancient, carved affair never designed to accommodate more than one person at a time, groaned audibly beneath the combined weight of two. But it served the purpose. With desire raging at fever pitch between them, a canvas army cot would have served the purpose.

He shed his clothes with impressive speed, but for the first time, he undressed her at delicious leisure, stripping away each item with dedicated control. Sophie felt the air of the April night cool on her naked flesh, then Dominic's hands charting her contours in mute fascination at the changes he found there.

"Wait," he begged when she tried to pull him down on top of her and reached out an arm to the bedside lamp. "Let me see you first." Rose-tinted light flooded the room, illuminating every inch of her to his absorbed gaze. "You are beautiful," he marveled, tracing a line from her breast to her softly rounded abdomen and resting his palm there.

The baby rolled over accommodatingly and kicked an acknowledgment. The pupils of Dominic's eyes flared, narrowing the irises to bands of dark, opaque green.

"Well, I'll be damned!" he breathed. "The little devil knows me! I had no idea—" he shook his head wonderingly "—no idea what to expect. I've never ... this is all new to me."

Helpless to prevent it, Sophie found her memory rewinding with chilling accuracy to another time two months before. *Guess what, darling. Miracle of miracles, I'm pregnant! We're going to have a baby, Dom!*

New? How could it all be new?

"Sophie?" Dominic touched her cheek. "Where have you gone?"

It was unfair to let the same old ghost displace her once again. Unfair and unthinkable. He had said Barbara was out of his life, that it was she, Sophie, who mattered.

"Nowhere," she whispered, sliding her hand from his ribs to his navel. Made bold by the rasping intake of his breath, she touched him, closing her fingers possessively around him in sultry emulation of intimacy. "I'm right here where I most want to be."

Sweat beaded his brow. "Just once," he said, holding himself very still, "I wanted to make love to you slowly...all night long...and kiss every inch of you...."

She tilted up her hips, nudging at his flesh with her own.

He slipped his finger between her thighs. "I wanted to watch the flush steal over your skin when I touched you here...like this...and told you things I should have told you long before now...."

She looked at him, all dusky in the lamplight, with the sheen of vitality that marked everything about him glowing in his eyes, and the need that had started to build from the minute he first touched her overflowed in a pool of molten heat, driven by hunger and the superstitious certainty that they'd be tempting fate to delay things any longer. As if only by joining their bodies in glorious defiance could they deflect any mischief the gods rained down on them.

"Dominic, please," she begged on a fractured cry. "The talking can wait...but I can't!"

CHAPTER EIGHT

HIS passion had never been more unreserved, his tenderness more profound, nor her response more intense. They achieved a harmony that night that surpassed the mortal and joined ranks with the divine. As if all those obstacles that once had seemed so insurmountable had been wiped away.

After, however, when Dominic had fallen into deep, jet-lagged sleep, the misgivings Sophie had repressed rose up again, threading along her nerve endings to sound distant chimes of alarm deep in her heart. Everything was falling into place too smoothly, too easily, and it wasn't meant to be this uncomplicated. Those things that really mattered never were.

When, in the murky light of dawn, he turned to her again, his mind still fogged with exhaustion but his body hungry, she snatched at borrowed happiness, riding passion's crest over and over again with a voracity whose aftermath left her weak and trembling. Because instinct warned her it might not last.

She crept from the bed just as the sun filtered through the plum blossoms to glint on the topmost windowpanes. In the remaining hour before Dominic awoke, she had time to shower and dress, plug in the coffeemaker and walk down to the bakery to pick up fresh rolls for breakfast.

"Something smells good," he said not long after she returned, and she looked up from setting a vase of forget-me-nots on the table to find him leaning over the banister watching her.

"Sweet rolls," she said, her heart lurching at the sight and sound of him. "And homemade cherry preserves."

"Cherry preserves, hmm? How'd you know they were my favorite?" He ambled across the room and, looping one hand around her neck, aimed a lingering kiss at her mouth as if he surely loved her, just a little bit.

If only he'd say so, perhaps the nagging anxiety would stop dogging her and she'd feel secure enough to tell him that she'd lied when she'd said she'd taken back her heart, that it was his to keep for the rest of time. But he'd never come close to such an admission, not even last night when, in the midst of scorching passion, he'd cried out her name and begged her never to leave him again. Why not? What hindrance deterred him from making that ultimate acknowledgment?

She slipped out of his embrace. "I didn't know they were your favorite. My next-door neighbor gave them to me as a housewarming gift when I moved in here."

"Ah, yes, the next-door neighbor! We met yesterday and were mutually unimpressed." He passed a rueful hand over his unshaven chin and broke into a grin. "Exactly how much does she know about me?"

So relaxed, so charming, so...*un*-Dominic! After the first time they'd made love, that afternoon on the island, he'd hardly been able to stand the sight of her. The second time, in his penthouse, he'd dropped her like a hot coal the minute Barbara showed up at the door. The ax was surely going to fall this time, too. The only question was, when.

"I told her everything I know, and it isn't very much— which brings us to the promise you made last night. I think I've lived with the questions long enough, Dominic. Now I'd like some answers."

The accusation in her voice sobered him. He sat down and gestured to the coffeepot. "Okay. Top me up with a quart of that, then fire away. Ask me anything at all."

Sophie filled his cup and began with the simplest. "How did you find me?"

"It wasn't difficult," he said, eyes narrowing slightly when she chose to sit in the chair opposite rather than the one beside him. "I went to see your parents. I was reluctant to do that at first in case you hadn't told them you'd gone missing, but it was obvious that they already knew and that they blamed me."

"That hardly explains how you tracked me down."

"Their attitude underwent a change when I told them you were pregnant and that I was not about to renege on my responsibilities to you or our child."

"You told my parents I'm expecting a baby?" Her other concerns overshadowed by this disclosure, Sophie stared at him, appalled. "Oh, you shouldn't have, Dominic! That's something they deserved to hear from me first."

He took a mouthful of coffee, then set down his cup very deliberately before replying, and she realized that the steel was still there beneath the engaging charm. "So why did you choose to leave them in ignorance, Sophie? It's not as if you didn't have plenty of time to fill them in on the facts."

She wriggled uncomfortably under his prolonged scrutiny. "I could hardly come out and say, 'I'm expecting and I've run off to lick my wounds because complications have arisen that make it seem unlikely that marrying the father is going to work out quite as simply as I'd hoped'."

"Why not? That's more or less how I put it to them, and they seemed to understand very well what I meant."

"They'd have been worried sick all these weeks!"

"They were anyway when you just upped and disappeared. Enough that it took very little persuasion on my part for them to tell me that your brother knew how to find you and for them to encourage me to come after you. Which," he added forcefully, "I had by then decided to do in any case, even if it meant hiring a private investigator to find you. Your folks weren't the only ones who were worried. Since speaking to them, I've had a few sleepless nights myself, wondering why you'd go to such lengths to keep the pregnancy secret, and I don't mind telling you, Sophie, I didn't much care for some of the reasons that occurred to me."

She didn't know what he meant by the latter part of his remark, nor did she much care just then. It seemed more to the point to inquire rather acidly, "Really? Is that why you waited over six weeks to come looking for me?"

He raised his eyebrows in mock confusion. "Your note stated quite emphatically that I'd rushed you into too many decisions since the start of the new year and that you needed time-out from all the pressure. If you didn't mean that, Sophie, why did you say it?"

"If you were all that worried about me, why didn't you ignore what I said and start searching for me sooner?"

"Because unlike you, my darling, I don't profess to know what's going on inside another person's head unless it's spelled out for me." There was no mistaking the exasperation creeping into his voice. "I'm told it's a common failing among men."

Sophie's intuition clicked into high gear. "Why do I get the feeling Barbara suddenly entered this conversation?"

"Because I apparently failed to 'understand' her, too." He slapped a generous spoonful of Violet's cherry preserve on his roll. "And I'm surprised it's taken you so long to bring up her name. I'd have thought you'd be more interested in clearing up the mystery of her disappearance more than four and a half months ago than in quibbling over petty details of the past few weeks. Don't you want to know the story behind her miraculous resurrection from the dead?"

Suddenly losing what little appetite she'd mustered, Sophie pushed away her plate with her sweet roll barely touched. The truth was, she wished they never had to mention Barbara's name again. She wished they could forget she'd ever existed. But her reappearance made it plain enough that she wasn't about to be so easily dismissed. "Not really," she admitted, "but not knowing is worse. So tell me, where did she spend the time and why did she let everyone think she'd drowned?"

"With the help of her boyfriend, she set the scene of her apparent demise, then disappeared with him to some neighboring island in order to 'discover' herself. Spouted a lot of rubbish about 'needing to make contact with her deep inner self before settling down', but the bottom line is, running barefoot through the sand with a lusty young lover promised to be a lot more exciting than marrying me. Until she realized how dependent she was on Visa, American Express, and all the comforts of home, that is. At which point she decided that life as a latter-day flower child in some third world speck of a country in the Caribbean wasn't quite her speed after all."

"I see," Sophie said. And she did, very clearly, although she might have had trouble believing anyone could be so callously irresponsible if she hadn't witnessed firsthand Barbara's utter disregard for anyone's interests but her own.

Dominic eyed her curiously. "You don't sound surprised by what I've told you. Care to explain why?"

"No."

His gazed sharpened. "Don't tell me you knew all along what she was up to!"

"Of course I didn't!" she exclaimed indignantly. "It's just that her behavior before her disappearance was rather... well, unusual."

"*Unusual*?"

"Yes."

"In that case," he said when she volunteered nothing further, "don't you think you should have passed along that information to the police at the time of her presumed death? It might have triggered a more thorough search, which in turn might have spared all of us, particularly the Wexlers, untold misery."

"The police knew. Everyone on St. Julian knew— except you."

"Knew *what*?"

She sighed unhappily. "Don't make me spell it out for you, Dominic. It—"

He'd been resting his chin on his fist, but at her obvious reluctance he slapped the flat of his hand on the table with such force that the cups danced in their saucers, slopping coffee everywhere. "Damn it, Sophie, stop beating around the bush! I've got a right to know. I was engaged to her."

"Precisely. And I don't want to be the one to shatter your illusions."

"Do you really think I've got any left where she's concerned?" he asked scornfully. "Come on, Sophie, spit it out. Obviously there were other men, but what else? Parties? Booze? Wild, antisocial behavior?"

She crumbled her roll into little pieces and pushed them around her plate with the tip of her forefinger. "That just about sums it up, yes."

"Why didn't you tell me at the time?"

She looked up from the mess she'd made. "You can't be serious! Good heavens, Dominic, you were so beside yourself with grief that you blamed me for her death. You certainly wouldn't have believed any attempt of mine to shift responsibility to her."

"Damn!" Abruptly, he shoved back his chair and paced the short distance to the window. For a while, he stood with his hands rammed in the back pockets of his pants and stared out at the clouds wheeling in from the west to obliterate great stretches of blue sky. She watched in silence. Finally, the unyielding line of his shoulders relaxed and he passed a weary hand down his face. "What the hell," he muttered, swinging back toward her, "this is crazy! I didn't come here to fight with you. I came to clear away all the garbage from the past that's driving a wedge between us and I guess the only way I can do that is to start at the beginning."

"I saw the beginning," Sophie reminded him tartly. "When I first started working on the Wexler project, I watched you with her, and even then I hated it. I don't think I want to relive it now."

"What did you see, Sophie?" Dominic asked, coming back to the table and snagging her fingers in his.

"A man in love."

He laughed dryly. "Funny how appearances can be deceiving, isn't it?"

She pulled her hand away. "If you're going to tell me you weren't smitten with her, Dominic, save your breath! It was obvious to anyone with eyes to see."

"You're right," he said bluntly. "I was in love with the whole idea of her. If I was the commoner who'd pulled himself up by the bootstraps, she was the princess. Where I'd had to claw my way to the top, she'd just floated. I was drawn to her glamour and energy and vitality, and by the time all that started to wear thin, other facets had come into play. I'd become one of the family, a son to the Wexlers, and I liked the feeling of belonging, of being needed. They knew Barbara was highly strung and saw in me a continuity of the stability they'd always provided. And without quite realizing when or how, I found myself taking over the role of protector. If it wasn't quite what I'd had in mind when I first proposed, other things that I hadn't expected made up for it."

"Are you saying you'd have married her just to please her parents and be accepted by them?" Sophie asked skeptically.

"I don't think I'd have recognized that was what I'd be doing." He reached for the coffeepot and refilled both their cups. "It's very easy to get comfortable enough in a situation to put up with its shortcomings, especially if, down the line, other things might come along to compensate."

"Like children, you mean?"

"Yes." He made no effort to dissemble. "I've always wanted children. That would have been a major factor in my decision to go through with the marriage, except..."

He paused and let his gaze roam over her face.

"Except what?"

"Except this leggy blond woman came to work on the estate. *Woman*, Sophie. Called herself a landscape architect but was really just a frustrated gardener who roamed around the place in dungarees, grubbing in dirt up to her elbows half the time, alongside her hired hands. She was hardworking and conscientious, and oh, Lord, was she kind to those old folks! Never too busy to stop and chat, never so full of herself that she couldn't spare the time to listen to their concerns."

He pinched the bridge of his nose. "Trouble was, the more I saw of her, the more I realized that Barbara was just a little girl playing at being grown-up, and no more cut out for marriage or motherhood than a boy is meant to shoulder a man's responsibilities."

Sophie fought against the flood of pleasure induced by his confession. "But you detested me on sight."

"I certainly tried hard enough. You made me question everything I was doing with my life. I found myself wondering what would have happened if I'd met you first." He raked the hair back from his forehead. "Crazy thoughts! Hell, you could have been married for all I knew."

"I'd never have guessed you felt that way. I found you so cold, so...suspicious. You acted as if you thought I might blow the place up when no one was looking. Every time I turned around, you were watching me."

A faint grin touched the corners of his mouth. "You'd better believe I was watching you! Do you know how delectable your backside is when you're bent over a flower bed?"

"You never even hinted—"

"I was scared spitless! Bad enough I was having serious second thoughts about sticking with my engagement without trying to start something with a woman I'd met through my future in-laws.'' He sighed. "Is any of this making sense to you?"

This was the man who'd once said with unshakable confidence, "I'm very single-minded...I don't give up and I don't back down...'' but for the first time he sounded unsure of himself. Yet although what he'd told her was unexpected, it made a certain sense and it definitely made him more human. She nodded. "More or less."

"Barbara must have guessed I was having doubts. She became edgy, more temperamental. Started testing me, picking fights over trifles, making scenes. Her folks were afraid she was headed for a breakdown of some sort. Apparently, she'd gone through some kind of emotional crisis the year before I met her and had threatened suicide. I felt like a jerk knowing that while they worried, all I cared about was finding a way to end things gracefully with the least amount of damage to everyone concerned. And then, as if she guessed what I had in mind, she took off to the Caribbean with you. And the next thing I knew, she was dead."

Sophie's heart filled with sympathy. She remembered the tortured expression on his face the day they'd driven out to the scene of the boat wreck, the agony she'd witnessed the afternoon he'd come to her hotel room to pack up Barbara's things, and for the first time she understood. If only he'd told her the truth then, how much pain they could have spared each other. But he was so good at presenting that cold, controlled front to the world, so very good at hiding his real feelings. "You felt guilty. Anyone would have."

"Guilty and, in a sick sort of way, relieved. The problem had been removed. I was free. And to make matters worse,'' he said, smothering a sigh, "there you were, very much alive. All sun-kissed apricot skin and warm, unselfish concern, worrying about me, trying to comfort me."

"You looked so torn up."

"I was! The idiot in me wanted to confess and throw himself on your mercy, the gentleman in me forbade it, and the lecher..." He shoved his fingers into his hair and ground the heels of his palms against his closed eyes. "Oh, the lecher drooled and fantasized and waited for the chance to cash in on a good thing, which happened sooner than I dared expect when you touched me that afternoon in the hotel room—"

"I couldn't help myself," Sophie cried. "You were so alone, so unhappy. And after, I thought how much you must despise me."

"Despise *you*?" He shook his head. "Hardly! All I could think was that the apple never falls far from the tree and that I had behaved no better than my father, a man for whom I had nothing but contempt. Yet even under those imperfect circumstances, making love to you exceeded anything I'd known with Barbara. That I was unlikely ever to have the pleasure of a repeat experience seemed fitting punishment."

"If you had only told me!" Sophie mourned.

"If you had only told me what had been going on before I arrived on the island!"

"What sort of woman would I be to have done a thing like that? You'd just lost your fiancée and were suffering enough. I wasn't about to make you feel any worse."

"No," he said wretchedly. "Your sort of woman would open her heart and her arms and give everything she had to make a man feel whole again. Which just brought home to me what I'd suspected all along—that you were my kind of woman.''

"Did it never occur to you that you might be my kind of man?"

"No. What would someone like you want with a morally bankrupt jerk like me?"

She got up and went to stand behind him. She leaned down and rested her chin against his thick, dark hair. He smelled of her soap, her shampoo. French lilac and mimosa, all mixed up with the scent of sheer masculine vitality. She loved him so much at that moment that she trembled from the force of it. It consumed her, body, mind and soul.

"You're not morally bankrupt, Dominic," she whispered, sliding her arms around his neck.

"Oh, yes, I am," he said, tilting back his head and trapping her in his clear green gaze. "When I found out you were pregnant, I saw my chance to nab you and I did, without a moment's hesitation. I'd been given a second chance and I wasn't about to blow it. The baby was the means, but you were the end."

Pregnant. The baby. Barbara.

They had yet to deal with the most serious issue of all. The realization slid into Sophie's consciousness just about the same time that Dominic reached up to draw her around his chair and onto his lap.

"I've covered up the truth for a long time, Sophie," he murmured in her ear, "but no more. I'll never lie to you again. You're everything I've ever wanted and I'll never let you go."

"Dominic," she said quickly, before the imperative quiver of her thigh beneath his hand erased the more urgent question in her mind, "what are we going to do about . . . ?"

He was kissing her, delicate, feathery kisses that stole up the side of her neck until they found her mouth. And his wicked, clever hand...oh, it had no scruples whatsoever, inching up her skirt in full view of anyone who might look in the window. "You're going to make an honest man of me as soon as possible," he informed her, misinterpreting her question, and kissed her again, deeply, erotically.

She snatched a shallow breath and fought against allowing her knees to fall slackly apart at the sweeping invasion of his hand. "Before I do," she said, "there's one very important point we've yet to discuss."

He nibbled at her ear, traced its inner curve with the tip of his tongue. His eyelashes flickered seductively against her cheek. "Can't it wait?"

"No." She pushed away his hand, straightened her skirt. "Dominic, what are you going to do about Barbara?"

His eyes snapped wide open, simmering with wry exasperation. "For crying out loud, sweetheart, not Barbara again—not now!"

"I have to know. We can't go on pretending she doesn't exist, especially not considering the circumstances."

He looked genuinely perplexed. "What circumstances? I told you, she and I are through. Finished. Done. She's probably got some other guy on her hook by now."

"But what about the baby?"

The amusement in his eyes died, extinguished by an emptiness that chilled Sophie to the bone. "There is no baby," he said.

"You mean she lied? She wasn't really pregnant?"

His expression turned hard, cold, cruel. "Oh, she was pregnant, all right. She had an abortion."

There it was at last, the thing Sophie had feared all along: the fatal flaw that would mar this new, too-perfect happiness. It hovered between them, a wicked, destructive thing made all the more ugly by Dominic's bald explanation.

With blinding hindsight, his offbeat remark about not caring for some of the ideas that had occurred to him when he learned that she hadn't told her parents about the baby, made sickening sense. That was what had prompted him to come looking for her: the fear that she'd run away to terminate her pregnancy, too, and that he stood to lose both his investments.

Sophie sprang to her feet, instinctively wrapping her arms around her middle in mute possession of her own child. "An abortion?"

"Yes. Sweetheart, you look as if you're going to pass out. Come back here and sit down."

"No!" Still clutching herself, she reeled away from him, around to the other side of the table, away from his beguiling, lying mouth.

Make an honest man of him?

It was enough to make her laugh!

He hadn't changed and he never would. He wanted a child, and once again, Barbara had outwitted him. So here he was, laying claim to his other investment. And because Sophie was so desperate for his love, she'd chosen to listen only to those things he said that fed her need when, in reality, he'd spent a far greater proportion of the relationship telling her things that denied it.

She doubled over, trying to contain the hysteria bubbling up.

He sprang from the chair, his face a mask of solicitous concern. "What's the matter, sweetheart? Is something wrong with the baby?"

She heard the sound of her own unlovely laughter. "Oh, *my* baby's just fine, thank you," she howled, clutching the back of a chair for support. "We both are. So why don't you get the hell out of my house and go home? Because neither of us needs you."

He rounded the table and made a grab for her. "What the devil's gotten into you, Sophie?"

Blindly, she lashed out. Caught him squarely on the jaw with one flailing fist, curved her fingers and went for his eyes with the other. And didn't care that in submitting to such behavior, she was violating one of her most dearly held principles. At that moment, she could have killed him.

He swung her around so that her back was to the table and bundled her unceremoniously against him, pinning her hands behind her back, plastering her breasts against his chest, trapping her legs between his. He subdued her with all the same moves he'd used to seduce her. Sexy, masculine. Deceitful, heartless.

"I don't know what you think I've done or said," he informed her flatly, "nor do I particularly care, but I'm damned if I'll stand idly by and let you use me as your personal punching bag."

She glared at him through the tears coursing down her face. He stared steadily back, his eyes at close range so utterly beautiful that she could hardly bear it. Why couldn't he have been as flawed on the outside as he was on the inside? It would have made him so much easier to resist in the first place.

Anguish swept through her, dissolving her rage. She sagged against him, not the way she had the night before, full of sensual entreaty, but in complete, crippling dejection. "Let me go," she said, her voice a pale echo of the apathy laying waste to her soul.

He released her. "Now what was all that about, Sophie?"

She turned away, amazed that the hollowness invading her hadn't robbed her of mobility. "I know why you're here, Dominic. Pretending to care about *me*, to want *me*."

"For crying out loud, if this is still about Barbara, I don't know how else to tell you that I *don't want her*."

"You don't want either of us," she said. "You want what we can give you. The difference is, she was smart enough to realize it a lot sooner than I was, and tough enough to know exactly how to thwart you."

"Exactly what are you saying, Sophie?" The question emerged loaded with warning.

She paid no heed. "You're a liar. Every word you say, every move you make, they're all calculated beforehand. You use them the same way you use money—as a disposable commodity to get you what you want."

"And just how did you reach that scintillating conclusion?"

"I took a long, hard look at the facts." She swiped at her tears, at the undignified dribbling of her nose. "You said it yourself not half an hour ago. You've been covering up ever since you met me, and you still are. No wonder you were so thrilled at how thoroughly pregnant I look! It would have been a real blow to discover you'd been robbed twice, wouldn't it? Because you didn't come after me. You came after your child. Well, enjoy the visit, Dominic, because I'll see you in hell before I let you get within a mile of him or me ever again."

With unruffled calm, he snapped one finger under the band of his watch so that the dial sat squarely in the center of his strong, elegant wrist. "You feel quite sure, do you, that you have sufficient evidence to make that decision?"

The inscrutability of his expression almost unnerved her. He had never seemed more remote, never more thoroughly veiled in that hauteur he was able to adopt with the flick of an eyelid. Then she remembered that this was all part of the disguise and that it was designed to set her off balance; to make her question her own judgment so that she'd more easily fall prey to his.

Marshaling herself to give an equally compelling performance, she said stonily, "Quite sure."

But she turned her back on him before she spoke, because otherwise her face would have betrayed her. The tears were welling up afresh, the grief contorting her features. How she held it all in check she didn't know.

He remained rooted to the spot, making no attempt to argue, to cajole her with a touch, an entreaty. At last, with the silence threatening to crack her composure to pieces, he moved.

He went up to the bedroom. She heard the creak of the floor above as he moved around. He came downstairs and opened the front door. She felt the brisk April breeze dance around her ankles.

"I hope you change your mind, Sophie," he said coldly. "I also hope you don't take too long to do it because I've just about run out of patience, and believe me, my darling, you'll like me even less when I play really dirty than you do when you just think I'm being a perfect bastard."

His measured stride rang out on the flagstone path of the courtyard. She heard the iron gate clang shut.

The emptiness that overflowed her heart exploded then, filling the room, the house, the rest of time.

He had gone from her life just as he'd come into it. With quiet, complete devastation. And the knowledge nearly killed her.

CHAPTER NINE

DOMINIC had known Grant Kaplan since high school. They'd played on the same football team and won identical scholarships to the same university. Circumstance had brought them together; shared ideals had made them friends.

When Grant got married the week after graduating from law school, Dominic had been his best man. Three years later, when the Kaplans outgrew the tiny apartment they'd rented shortly after the wedding, and no other landlord in town was interested in leasing to a couple with a fourteen-month-old toddler and another baby on the way, it never occurred to them to turn to anyone but Dominic to build them a house they could afford.

Five weeks after Dominic came back from England with steam pouring out of his ears and decided to set in motion the wheels of justice as they pertained to custody of his child, he naturally went to his old college buddy, Grant Kaplan, who by then had earned the deserved reputation of being one of the hottest lawyers in town.

When Dominic learned there wasn't much he could do to enforce his paternal rights until after the baby was born and that, even then, Sophie still had the upper hand as long as she remained abroad, he did exactly what he'd promised her he would do if she didn't change her attitude. In true bastard fashion, he instructed Grant to put the squeeze on her.

Grant chewed the end of his pen, the same disposable plastic type he'd always favored, and subjected Dominic to what he probably thought was an insightful stare.

"Are you sure this is the route you want to take, pal? It's not the sort of action likely to improve your relationship, no matter what the motivation, and what good is victory if you can't take any pride in the way you went about achieving it?"

"Draw up the papers and stop playing pop psychologist," Dominic snarled.

"Have you tried talking to her? Explaining—"

Dominic swore colorfully.

"Very good," Grant commended him when the expletives finally ran dry. "Now, to repeat the question—"

"How do I talk to someone who consistently refuses to hear what I'm saying and whose sole reaction to the slightest hint of trouble is to freeze me out and put as many goddamned miles between us as possible? So don't bother repeating that she's legally free to live wherever she chooses and that if I want to exercise my parental rights I'll have to wait until after the baby's born and then go through the British court system, because I've no intention of sitting around on my butt waiting for her to disappear again. I want her brought back here before she gives birth, and if playing dirty is the only way I can do it, I'll play dirty. It'll come as no great surprise to her, believe me."

"She could end up hating you."

"She already hates me. I hate her. Hell, we hate each other!"

"Yes. Well, that certainly explains how the two of you ended up in the sack together and why you've tried so hard to coerce her into marriage."

"Draw up the papers," Dominic advised him darkly, "and save the funny stuff for someone who appreciates it."

*   *   *

"You look like a pregnant Joan of Arc waving the rebel flag," Paul said when Sophie paid a visit early in July. "Sit down and take a load off your swollen ankles. Screaming at me isn't going to change anything."

"I thought you'd be on my side," Sophie raged. "I expected it."

Paul, who'd taken to smoking a pipe and affecting all sorts of other donnish British customs, tamped down his tobacco and replied placidly, "It's not a matter of taking sides, Sophie. It's a matter of what's best for you and ultimately for the baby. And rampaging around the West Country in your little Mini-Minor hardly fits the bill. Anyway, I rather liked your Dominic."

Jenny beamed. "So did I."

"He's not my Dominic," Sophie fumed. "I wouldn't take him if he was the last man on earth."

"Just as well," Paul said, "because the way you're going about things, you aren't going to get him. What did you do, for crying out loud, to bring out the savage in him like this?"

"I called him a liar to his face. Which he is."

"Are you sure?"

"Of course I'm sure! He followed me over here and tried to convince me he wanted to take me home and marry me!"

Paul nodded through clouds of pungent smoke. "I can see why you'd find that very hard to believe," he remarked cheerfully.

Sophie could have strangled him. It was shocking, in fact, how frequently her thoughts had turned to violence since the letter had arrived, although she supposed it was preferable to the dreadful apathy that had hounded her ever since Dominic Winter walked out on her.

She'd known that a person couldn't go on indefinitely skipping meals and taking refuge in sleep, but she'd certainly given it a royal try. Anything had been better than trailing through the long summer days, reliving useless regrets.

Violet had been very worried. "You don't look well, lass," she'd said. "Are you going in for regular checkups at the clinic?"

She had been. Sort of. But the lineups were often long, and occasionally she got a peculiar sensation low down in her womb, a sort of pressure that, while it wasn't painful, was rather disquieting. So, depending on how she was feeling, she sometimes stayed home and lay on a chaise in the back garden, reading books that were just as good as prenatal classes at preparing her for childbirth.

Besides, it was very hard being around happy expectant mothers who more often than not had doting husbands in tow. Sophie didn't need the reminder that she was alone. She never forgot it even for a moment, and she never stopped hurting over it.

"What am I going to do about this?" she demanded, waving the letter under Paul's nose again. "You've read what's in it. What do you think?"

"That either you go home and call a cease-fire while the pair of you sort out your differences, or you'll wind up flat broke. And in view of your condition, the latter seems a trifle inconvenient."

He'd mastered the British art of understatement, too. He'd be wearing academic robes and keeping an old English sheepdog next! "It just goes to prove that Dominic Winter's every bit as rotten as I thought," she spat. "What kind of man would deliberately reduce the mother of his child to insolvency?"

"The kind you're in love with, obviously," Paul said to Jenny's tittering approval. "Good Lord, Sophie, why don't you stop working yourself into a lather and just go and talk to the guy? He didn't strike me as all that unreasonable."

The fact was, she'd known in her heart that she'd reacted hastily and perhaps even unfairly to Dominic. She'd been ready to cave in and try to make amends, if not for her own sake then for their child's. Until this, his latest attempt to bend her to his will, had been delivered to her door. Now she'd rather die than give him the satisfaction!

"I should have taken his money and run with it when I had the chance," she lamented. "He's the one who wanted to pay off my mortgage at the bank, but I thought it'd make me feel less as if I was being bought if he became the lender of record instead. I insisted we have an official agreement drawn up—and look where it's landed me!"

"Up the creek without a paddle," Paul concluded wittily. "Or, more accurately, hugely in debt and divested of your home, because there's no doubt he can sell off the property to recover his losses on the house he custom-built for you."

"And this is the man who swore he'd never renege on his fatherly obligations!"

"He's not. All he's asking—"

"Demanding! He never *asks* for anything."

Briefly, Paul forgot he fancied himself as a sober academic and sniggered into his teacup.

Jenny rushed to keep the peace. "All he wants is for you to show up in person, Sophie, and sign an agreement spelling out his visitation rights and the child support payments he's prepared to make."

"He's blackmailing me."

"And managing to keep his integrity intact while he does it," Paul said, recovering himself. "I must admit I rather admire him."

Sophie stared at him, dumbfounded. "You're not going to help me, are you?"

He fiddled around with his damnable pipe again. "If by that you mean am I going to meddle in something that's none of my affair, the answer is no, I'm not. I do not relish ending up in the cross fire between a man and a woman who are being kept apart by something that, to my mind, might be easily and quickly resolved if you, my dear sister, would swallow your pride long enough to ask Dominic one very simple question."

"Oh, really," she said, dangerously miffed. If it hadn't been for Jenny, who kept stroking her back as if she were an overbred cat refusing fresh cream, she'd walk out. It was the one thing she'd practiced rather often of late and she was becoming quite good at it. "And what question is that, my dear brother?"

"You know that this Barbara person was pregnant. You know she had an abortion."

"So?"

"Did you ever bother to determine if the child she carried was Dominic's?"

Sophie felt her jaw drop, and just for a fleeting, glorious moment, hope soared. Then reality returned with a thud. "I was there when she made the announcement. I heard her say, '*We're* going to have a baby'."

"And you believed her?"

"Why wouldn't I?"

"Considering that you now know the lengths to which she'll go to have her way, why would you? She lied about everything else, didn't she? What's to say she didn't try to pass off her lifeguard lover's child as Dominic's? And what if Dominic knew from the outset that there was no way the child could be his? What if it never entered his mind that *you'd* believe it, either?"

What if, indeed! It provided considerable and provoking food for thought, especially since not a hint that she might be pregnant had once passed Barbara's lips. In view of how free she'd been with her other confidences, it hardly seemed likely she'd have kept quiet about something as momentous as a baby in the making.

"If the baby had been Dominic's," Jenny put in thoughtfully, "that would mean she was already pregnant when she went down to the Caribbean with you at the end of November, and she'd be at least fourteen weeks along by the time she showed up again in Palmerstown. You saw her, Sophie. Did she look pregnant to you?"

"She looked the way she always did, skinny as a reed."

"It all adds up if you ask me," Paul said, puffing complacently on his damned pipe.

"Yes," Sophie said meekly. "Now that you mention it, I suppose it does."

Paul shrugged. "Then instead of spinning your wheels over here, book the next possible flight to Vancouver and find out, Sophie. And don't take too long to do it. It's the height of the tourist season, seat space is at a premium, and you've only got until August the fifteenth to sign on the dotted line if you don't want to lose your house."

She must have looked even more churned up than she felt. The flight attendant swept a keen, professional eye over her, tucked her ticket stub to one side and, as soon as the Air Canada jet had reached cruising altitude, moved her to business class where, in addition to being wider and reclining farther, the seats came equipped with little footrests that afforded divine relief to Sophie's swollen, eight-month-pregnant ankles.

She was plied with extra pillows, another blanket, an early lunch. After, while the rest of the passengers watched a movie, she tried to sleep. But every time she closed her eyes, the same unlikely scenario played itself out: what if Paul had alerted Dominic to the fact that she was coming home, and when she cleared customs in Vancouver, he was waiting to sweep her into his arms?

What if, in between breathtaking kisses, he confirmed what she now suspected, that the other baby hadn't been his, and Barbara's decision to end the pregnancy had had nothing to do with him?

Just like before, though, it was too easy a solution to bear up under pressure. Problems didn't solve themselves so neatly. The difference was that this time Sophie was prepared for disappointment and therefore not overly surprised to find no one waiting to greet her amid the mob of people waiting to meet the flight.

Within the hour, she was on the road in the car she'd rented for the last leg of her journey, the long and arduous drive into the southern interior. She drove until early evening, then stopped for the night in a motel. It seemed a smart idea, especially as she was again conscious of that low abdominal pressure.

Once this latest mess was sorted out—if it ever was— she really would have to devote more time to taking better care of herself and the baby. She had exactly four weeks in which to conclude her business with Dominic and find a place to live. Unless...

She shook her head impatiently. It was too late for unlesses and what ifs. She and Dominic might have begun their relationship in the bedroom, but it was ending in a courtroom. Not a very auspicious sign!

The temperature was hovering around ninety the next afternoon when she drove over the mountain pass and down into the blistering heat of the valley. The dry, semidesert air hit like a blast furnace, scorching her lungs and turning the steering wheel tacky beneath her hands.

She could have pared fifteen minutes off the final lap of her journey if she'd taken the upper highway from there, but she turned the other way, along the narrower, quieter lakeshore route, past the place that had once been home. It was cooler down by the water and it wasn't as if anyone was expecting her. She was coming home the same way she'd left—unexpectedly.

The road unrolled in front her, distorted by heat waves. In the orchards on either side, the last of the peach crop hung ripe and golden from the trees. Up on the hills, the vineyards were heavy with fruit.

Even with all the windows rolled down, the car was still unbearably hot. It was another typical August day in the southern interior: somnolent, windless and glaringly bright. She could taste the dust in her throat, feel her clothes sticking to the leather upholstery of the car.

She hadn't intended to slow down at the turnoff to the rutted driveway that led to the site of her old house. It was more as if the car had a will of its own and wasn't about to take direction from her.

There was no sign of life about the place; nothing new or different at all, in fact. The grove of fruit trees remained undisturbed by all the supposed changes while the broad leaves of the huge old maple drooped listlessly in the blistering heat. Everything looked just the same. Until she rounded the last bend and saw the house he'd built for her.

It didn't sprawl exactly; it was much too elegant. Instead, it reclined on the long, grassy slope above the lake as if, when God made the earth, He'd had this particular spot in mind for just such a dwelling.

Killing the engine, Sophie remained behind the wheel of her car and simply stared through the windshield, dry-mouthed with admiration. Whatever else he didn't do right, Dominic knew how to design and build a house. Sunshine dazzled its white stucco walls and blue tiled roof. Tall, gleaming windows soared to deep, protective eaves. A flight of shallow, curving steps led up to double front doors with etched-glass inserts.

She couldn't resist a closer investigation. Nudging the car door closed with her hip, she walked up the steps, pressed her nose to the nearest window and knew right away she wouldn't be satisfied simply to look.

She tried the front doors, found they were unlocked and, like Alice, stepped into a wonderland of pale hardwood floors, twelve-foot ceilings and deep moldings. There was a kitchen with granite countertops and a breakfast bar; a dining room big enough to entertain royalty; a nursery with a built-in intercom. Entranced, she walked quietly down the hall, passing spacious rooms flooded with sunshine and shimmering reflections from the lake.

French doors stretching the width of the back of the house gave access to a brick-paved patio. From there, a path wound down to the water. To either side, mounds of topsoil waited for the landscaper to restore the flower beds that had been disturbed by all the construction. Sophie itched to get down on her knees, bury her hands in the rich loam and bring the garden back to brilliant life.

At the foot of the property, the lake lapped indolently against the shore. Farther out, the surface of the water lay smooth as glass. Picking her way carefully, Sophie crossed the rock-strewn strip of beach and, without bothering to remove her sandals, waded up to her ankles in the relatively cool shallows.

It felt so good to be home again.

And then she heard it floating across the somnolent air of midafternoon: the unmistakable growl of a vehicle cruising up the driveway from the road. If it was Dominic returning...oh, she couldn't face the indignity of his catching her snooping around and looking like an oversize pumpkin in a travel-creased tent!

Splashing ashore, she cut across the beach at an angle to avoid being seen from the patio, intending to sneak away up the side of the property. But her eyes were dazzled from the glare of the water, her leather-soled sandals slick on the sunbaked rocks. She blundered forward, her mind fixed on escape at any price, and felt her ankle twist out from under her.

Clutching at thin air, she skidded, lost her footing and landed hard astride a huge boulder. She blinked at the moment of jarring pain, seemed to hear each vertebra crunch against its neighbor. Slithering to the sand, she rotated her ankle and gingerly tested her weight on it.

Miraculously, no bones appeared to be broken. And yet... something wasn't quite right. Something had torn loose inside, where her baby was supposed to remain safely cocooned for another four weeks. That feeling of pressure was back, more persistent, more ominous than ever. Every instinct urged her to remain still in order to minimize whatever problem was manifesting itself.

"Help!" she cried, her throat aching and her heart unraveling with fear.

Her voice floated up into the thick, hot air and was met by drowsing silence. The sun beat down mercilessly. A flicker of pain stabbed the small of her back. And in the distance she heard the sound of the Jaguar's engine fading down the driveway, heard it slow down as it met the junction with the road, then take off with a roar of power in the direction of town.

Forgetting all the things she'd read about, she tensed, helpless to control either her body or her mind. No one had answered her cry for help and she didn't need a book to tell her that her baby was coming, uncaring that it was too early and that his mother was alone on a deserted stretch of beach.

The pain had subsided to a persistent ache, but a sense of urgency gripped her. She was in labor and she had to make it back to the house while she still had the strength, to the kitchen where she remembered seeing a phone on the breakfast bar.

Cradling her belly in her hands, she stumbled forward and tried not to think of the number of steps she'd have to take to reach her objective. She was only halfway home when the first contraction hit.

With a monumental effort at control, she breathed deeply. She must not panic, even though she was helpless to govern the order of events or the speed at which they were occurring. Emptying her mind of all but the urgency of dragging her reluctant body up to the house, she navigated the last of the rocky shore with excruciating care and determination.

Rough-hewn cedar steps with a single railing spanned the drop from garden to beach. She hauled herself up the first two well enough, but as she attempted the third, another contraction clamped hold and something flooded warm and thick between her thighs.

She knew instinctively that what was happening to her was not a normal part of labor. Things were happening too quickly and in the wrong order. This was not the beginning of birth but a slow sort of death for her baby.

"Dominic!" she wailed softly, tears filming her eyes.

She had threatened never to let him know his child, but she hadn't meant it. She would never have punished him like that. She loved him. She loved him and she needed him. But she'd left it too late to let him know. Because if their baby died, he would neither believe her nor forgive her.

Their baby would not die. She would not allow it.

Gritting her teeth, she pressed on, shutting out the dizzying pain, the blinding sun, the endless, endless path, and at last the French doors that looked out on the patio were a hand's grasp away. From somewhere beyond the fear, she scraped up the energy to wrestle them open, to drag herself over the threshold and across the floor to the breakfast bar.

She'd made it. She was home.

Her hand reached for the phone, closed around the cord, pulled it toward her. Then the last of her strength gave out, and with a sigh she sagged against the side of the bar and slid all the way down to the smooth oak floor, taking the receiver with her.

Dominic jumped down from the truck to check on the unfamiliar car parked at the foot of the steps, saw the purse lying on the front seat with a ticket stub tucked into the side pocket and knew at once who the unexpected visitor was.

"Don't bother waiting," he told his foreman. "I'll lock the place up and hitch a ride back into town with my guest."

As soon as the truck disappeared down the driveway, he leaped up the steps and into the house because he'd thought at first that that was where she'd be, especially when he noticed the front door standing open.

When he didn't find her there and there was no answer when he called out her name, he raced back outside again, struck suddenly by the thought that she could drive away while his back was turned. It would be just like her to sneak off before they had a chance to straighten out the ridiculous mess they'd managed to get themselves into.

Her car was exactly where she'd left it and he was running in circles, so bloody exhilarated that she was back that he wasn't thinking straight! She was probably hiding somewhere in the garden, enjoying watching him make an ass of himself. Well, he'd fix her wagon. Literally!

Sauntering over to the car, he reached inside, removed the key from the ignition and tossed it into the bushes. Then he strolled up the steps and went back into the house. He'd wait and let her come to him for a change because neither of them was going anywhere until she did.

It wasn't easy to be patient. He'd missed her badly. As the days had passed, all the aggression he'd nurtured had faded into one long, aching need that flared wild and unruly through his veins.

He didn't care anymore that she'd hurt him with her accusations, or angered him with her threats. All he wanted was to hold her, feel the reality of her in his arms, the substance of her close to his heart. He wanted to touch her and tell her that he loved her and that if he had his way they'd never spend another night apart.

He ambled down the long hall, looking into each room as he passed, just in case he'd missed her the first time around. Had she liked the nursery? The master suite? The nanny's quarters?

He passed by the dining room and pushed open the swinging door to the kitchen, the heart of every house he built. And felt his own heart stammer to an agonizing halt when he saw her crumpled in a heap next to the breakfast bar.

The universe narrowed to her closed eyes, the sharp angle of her cheekbones. Dropping to his knees beside her, he scooped her into his arms, shocked at her pallor and appalled at her fragility.

"Sophie," he whispered brokenly, rocking her to and fro. "Sophie...my darling, my love, what have you done to yourself?"

When he saw the stain on her hyacinth blue dress, he at first refused to acknowledge what it had to be and tried to pretend his eyes were deceiving him. But nothing changed, no matter how fiercely he blinked. Sophie was hemorrhaging.

"Hold on, sweetheart," he told her. "I'll get you to Palmerstown General before you know it."

Except that he had no means of taking her there. The key to the car was buried in waist-high shrubbery because he had been so anxious, once again, to show her who wielded the power.

Cursing, he secured the phone in the angle of his shoulder and dialed the emergency number. Heard himself barking out directions to find the house. But all that really registered were Sophie's pale, drawn features and the terrible dread that in pushing for what he wanted, he'd finally gone too far.

This was not the way to write their ending, with her dying in his arms. They had too much loving to share.

Emergency vehicles arrived within half an hour, their various sirens splintering the stillness of the afternoon. Swift, efficient men in white poured into the kitchen and took charge. They bundled her onto a gurney, wheeled her outside to a waiting ambulance and took her away. Dominic sat beside her, holding her limp hand to his cheek, willing her to hold on, to take all his strength and use it for herself.

They hung tubes from her arms, pierced the softness of her skin with needles, fed her oxygen. A young paramedic bent over her, an intent stranger with his alien hand on her stomach, listening through a stethoscope to the baby's heart.

"Never mind the child," Dominic snarled, beside himself at being reduced to the role of helpless spectator. "Listen to *her* heart—save *her* life."

"Calm down, buddy," the paramedic advised laconically. "We don't aim to lose either one."

Murderous rage rose up in Dominic. What did this cocky young bastard know?

Enough to keep his attention where it belonged.

Chagrined, Dominic followed suit. "Sweetheart," he whispered, kissing the hand he held in his. "Sweetheart..."

Miraculously, she opened her eyes. He lifted his head and saw she was looking at him, that she was radiant. "Dominic," she murmured, smiling like an angel through the pain. "I needed you and you came."

"Of course I did," he replied huskily, the emotion almost choking him. "Where do you get off trying to cheat me out of being here for my son's birth?"

"What if she's a girl?"

"Not a chance," he said. "We're starting our own football team. Anyhow, girls are always late. She wouldn't have finished packing yet."

Her smile faltered and beads of sweat popped out on her forehead. She gripped his hand with bone-crushing force. "Ohhh," she gasped, drawing in a great breath. "Are we nearly there?"

The paramedic caught Dominic's eye and nodded. "Just about," he said, "and we've radioed ahead. They're expecting us."

He sounded calm. But he looked anxious.

CHAPTER TEN

THE worst thing about hospitals, Dominic concluded savagely, as the congregation of personnel attending Sophie huddled for another whispered conference, was that everyone from the most junior clerk in admissions to the head nurse on the maternity floor seemed part of one great conspiracy to keep people like himself firmly on the outside.

"No, I'm not her husband," he snarled when they tried to shoo him out of the cubicle where they had Sophie cloistered. "I'm her lover and that's my baby she's about to deliver. So don't tell me that what goes on here is none of my business because I'm making it my business, damn it!"

"You don't make the rules around here," the iron-faced head nurse informed him severely. "In fact, you don't have any clout at all. So unless you want to find yourself booted out of this unit, please lower your voice."

Only Sophie, clutching his hand and whimpering softly, kept him from firing back a retort that would likely have landed him behind bars.

"That's better." The nurse nodded approvingly. "Now, I need to get some consent forms signed. Feel up to doing that for me, Sophie? Time is of the essence since that baby of yours is in such a hurry to make an appearance."

"Give them to me," Dominic said, reaching for the clipboard. "She's got enough to deal with."

Old Hatchet-face slapped his hand away. "You're not eligible. If the patient isn't able to sign, we'll have to send for the next of kin."

"Please don't do that," Sophie begged. "I can sign."

"Wonderful. Dr. Overby just arrived and will be in to see you as soon as we've finished the paperwork."

"This man Overby," Dominic said, chasing the nurse out of the cubicle, "how good is he?"

She favored him with a fishy-eyed glare. "Count your blessings, Mr. Winter. From the looks of it, Ms. Casson's going to need the best and fortunately that's what she'll be getting."

Dominic didn't like the sound of that. He liked even less the sober expression on the specialist's face when he came out to the waiting area after completing his examination of Sophie.

"You're the father of Ms. Casson's baby, I understand," he said, approaching Dominic.

"Yes. And her fiancé."

"I see. Well, I'm afraid we're looking at surgery, Mr. Winter."

The words rang with a foreboding that made Dominic's skin crawl. "What sort of surgery?"

"A cesarean section—something I normally try to avoid."

Dominic couldn't get used to the idea of not being in charge. It went against the grain to be at the mercy of someone else's judgment, especially a stranger's. "Then avoid it now."

"That's not possible," the doctor said firmly. "I'm sorry."

Suddenly, Dominic wasn't a thirty-five-year-old man; he was a kid again, standing in another hospital like this and listening to another doctor tell him that his mother was dying and there was nothing anyone could do about it. "Why not?" he'd asked, his seventeen-year-old heart aching, because he'd known that, if she hadn't been saddled with him, her life might have turned out differently. "Why not?" he asked now, his heart nearly breaking. "Is it my fault?"

The doctor's gaze softened. "No one's to blame, son. She's very narrow through the pelvis and you..." He indicated Dominic's breadth of shoulder. "Well," he said dryly, "it wouldn't have been easy under the best of circumstances. But there are unforeseen complications."

Dominic felt the ground rock under him. "Complications?"

"Unless we intervene, I'm afraid that she'll deliver the placenta first and that could cost us the baby."

"How dangerous is this surgery?"

"All surgery's serious, but..." The doctor shrugged. "It's routine procedure."

There was nothing routine about someone taking a knife to his Sophie! "Listen," he said, "Sophie comes first. Do whatever you must, but if it comes down to a choice, save her and let the baby go. There'll be other children but..." He stopped, almost choking in the effort not to break down. "But there'll never be another Sophie."

They had given her something that filled her with rainbows. She floated just out of reach, aware of what was happening around her but not a part of it.

She smiled. From beyond the thin wall of the cubicle, Dominic's voice rose in frustration. He was having such a hard time taking orders for a change, instead of dishing them out....

"...her fiancé," he said. She liked the sound of that. "...my fault," he said, and she heard the agony in his voice and wished they'd give him something for his pain, too. "...Sophie comes first...save her and let the baby go."

Let the baby go?

Never, she thought hazily. *The baby is my gift to you, my darling.*

The curtains rustled and she knew he was beside her again. She felt his strong fingers close around hers, felt his lips against her cheek. "They're taking you upstairs in a minute, but I'll be down here waiting, sweetheart," he said. "I'll always be here, no matter what."

The rainbows spread, swirling through her mind and taking her away.

"Look at it this way," Old Hatchet-face had told him when they wheeled Sophie into the elevator. "You'll be spared all that pacing up and down the halls. It'll be over before you know it."

Not so. Distracted, Dominic glanced at the wall clock for the fortieth time in as many minutes. He'd paced miles, waited centuries, and still there was no word. Her room was ready, the high, narrow bed with its stark linens mocking him with its emptiness.

As empty as his life would be without her, he thought, his heart swelling painfully. She eased his most vital hunger, answered his most quiet need. She was his whole world.

Behind him, the elevator doors whispered open. "You have a son, Mr. Winter."

It was like a television drama. The doctor stood there wearing his silly green hat, a mask dangling around his neck, his shapeless green suit and boots making him look like one of the seven dwarfs after a hard day in the gold mine.

"A son?" Was that his voice cracking? And why, for Pete's sake, were the geometrical proportions of the hall blurring? He hadn't cried when his mother died, and he'd been only a kid then. "A son...!" And he a father with the tears running down his face for all the world to see. "What about my fiancée, my Sophie?"

"Take a look for yourself."

Rubber wheels swished from behind. Swiping at his face with the cuff of his sleeve, he looked down and saw she was smiling in her sleep, the lightest flush staining the hollows of her cheeks, and so delicate under the sheets that she looked little more than a child herself.

"Sophie?" he whispered, and miracle of miracles, she heard him. Her eyes opened and focused on him.

"It's going to be a football team, Dominic," she murmured drowsily. "They were all out of little girls."

Of course, it would have been easy to wallow in the euphoria and forget there'd ever been a cross word exchanged between them.

"After all, Sophie," her mother had said, beaming down at her new grandson the next afternoon, "you and Dominic are together again. He stayed with you all last night, despite everything the hospital staff did to try to evict him, and look at the beautiful flowers he sent. Obviously, whatever the problems were, this little fellow's banished them. So why don't you put the past behind you and enjoy your little son?"

"Problems don't go away because you ignore them, Mother. Dominic and I still need to sort out a few things."

"They can wait until you're home and settled down again."

But where was home?

"I'd make it clear it's wherever he hangs his hat—not to mention his pants," Elaine declared when she stopped by that afternoon after work to meet her godson. "For heaven's sake, don't keep adding to your misery! The most gorgeous guy this side of heaven's built you a mansion, he's the father of this adorable, wrinkled creature, and you love him. I should be half as lucky!''

The baby stretched, waved a tiny fist in the air and let out a screech of protest. "Just like his daddy." Sophie smiled. "Less than twenty-four hours old and already expecting to run the show."

"Ganging up on me already?" Dominic inquired from the doorway.

"Oops! Time I was out of here." Elaine scooped up her bag and planted a kiss on the baby's head. "Nice seeing you again, Dominic," she said in passing, "and congratulations."

Even after she'd gone, Dominic continued to hover on the threshold as though unsure of his welcome. "Come on in and say hello to your son," Sophie suggested.

He half shrugged and deposited a huge bunch of white lilies on the foot of her bed before going to stand over the bassinet. Sophie watched him reach out a long, tanned finger and saw the look on his face when the baby grabbed ahold.

"Wouldn't you like to hold him, Dominic?" she asked softly.

He shuffled his feet uneasily and closed big awkward hands around the tiny bundle. "I'm not sure I know how."

"Then you'd better learn," she said. "Unless, of course, you plan to leave me to do all the work of caring for him."

He lifted the baby clear and cradled him against his chest. "Isn't that what you said you wanted, Sophie?"

"Oh, Dominic," she sighed, wishing he'd just come and put his arms around her, as well, instead of keeping such a safe distance between them, "we've managed to say so many things to each other that we didn't mean.

What I accused you of when you came to see me in Wells, what I said about Barbara . . ."

He looked at her over the top of his son's head. "It wasn't my baby, Sophie. There was no way it could have been and I knew that right away."

She dipped her head. "I guessed as much."

"I shouldn't have left you guessing. I shouldn't have pressured you into coming home." He heaved a great sigh and tucked the baby back in the bassinet. "I've done and said nothing but the wrong thing ever since I met you and I never meant things to be like that."

"Did you mean it last night when I heard you say, 'let the baby go'?"

He looked down at their child again, his eyes full of pain. "Yes. But that was last night and I thought I might lose you. Now, today, I have a son and I can't unwish him. We hardly know each other, yet already I love him."

And what about me? Sophie longed to ask. *Do you love me, too*?

Outside the window, the sunbaked hills rose above Palmerstown. The waters of Jewel Lake shone blue and aquamarine beneath another cloudless sky. And across the room, Dominic looked at her with eyes the color of jade. "I'll never try to take him away from you, Sophie, I promise. I'll do whatever you ask, but please, let me see him once in a while. Let me know my boy."

"Is that all, Dominic?" she asked, her voice breaking. "Is there nothing else you'd like to say to me?"

"There's nothing else I can say, except I'm sorry."

That wasn't all he could say! It would be so easy to set everything right between them if only he could tell her the one thing she most needed to hear. But he had turned away and was staring out of the window at the melon-colored tones of early sunset tinting the western sky.

"I'm sorry, too," she said quietly, "because I don't know where to go from here."

He pivoted toward her, looking as close to shamefaced as she ever expected to see him. "All my talk about repossessing the house was just so much hot air, another example of my not knowing when to keep my mouth shut. The house is yours if you want it, you know that."

"And what do you want, Dominic?"

He shook his head and the expression in his beautiful eyes undid her. He had never looked more vulnerable or uncertain. "I want you," he said. "You're all I've ever wanted. I love you."

Just that. The simplicity of it knocked everything else—the hurt, the loneliness, the doubt—clean out of her head and into the past where it belonged. "Oh, Dominic, then that's all that matters because I love you, too."

He stared at her unbelievingly. "But how can you? After everything—the way I am, the business with the house—"

"I don't care about the house!" she cried, holding out her arms to him. "Don't you know that I could live in a shoe box and be happy as long as you're there to share it with me?"

"I'll try to change, to be a better person—"

"No. I love *you*, Dominic."

"Enough to marry me?"

"More than enough."

The beginnings of a smile illuminated his eyes and softened the sober line of his mouth.

"Thank God!" he breathed, and finally took the first step in the last two yards that separated them. "*Thank God!*"

The baby let out a squawk of annoyance just then, as though to remind them that he was supposed to be the star of the show.

Midway between the bed and the bassinet, Dominic stopped and looked at Sophie uncertainly. "Do I have to pick him up again?"

She laughed. "You might as well get used to it, Dominic. I have the feeling he's going to be just as demanding as his daddy."

"Maybe he's hungry." Dominic made a face. "Or wet. Listen, Sophie, I'm not sure I'm going to be much help when it comes to diapers and that sort of thing."

"You'll learn," she said. "We'll learn together, about all sorts of things. Bring our son here, Dominic, and let's get started."

He carried the baby to her and perched beside her on the bed. "I want to hold you, but I'm afraid of hurting you," he said, sliding a tentative arm around her shoulders.

She lifted her face to his. "I could stand being kissed without experiencing too much discomfort."

His lips hovered over hers. "I will never disappoint you again," he murmured against her mouth.

"Oh, Dominic," she sighed, leaning into his embrace, "all that matters is that we love each other and our son, don't you know that?"

He kissed her then, a deep, possessive kiss. It might have lasted the rest of the night if the baby hadn't let out another outraged squawk.

"He's got quite a set of lungs," his father observed.

"He needs to be fed," his mother replied. "He also needs a name."

"How about Tiger?"

"How about Screecher?"

"Do you want to name him after your family?"

"I want to name him for ours, yours and mine. Let's choose something fresh to mark our brand-new beginning."

"Before we do that," Dominic said, running a loving hand through her hair as she settled the baby at her breast, "let's choose a wedding date. He might as well understand from the beginning that sometimes we come first."

hand brought the knife to one settled the only at last
breast. "Let's change a subject a personal to as
so understood from his reminders that so always at
colar over.

EPILOGUE

THEY decided on a Christmas wedding.

"Business is pretty quiet in December," Dominic said when they put the idea to Sophie's parents. "We'll be able to take a nice, long honeymoon."

"And by then the baby won't need to be fed quite as often," Sophie said, referring to the fact that in the weeks immediately following his birth, Ryan demanded meals at regular two-hour intervals.

Sophie's mother was ecstatic. "It's the perfect time! Paul and Jenny are coming home for Christmas anyway, and we'll have a full three months to organize something lavish."

"Lavish?" Sophie's father echoed. "I'd have thought discreet was a better choice, considering they've both done everything backward. In my day, a man usually married a woman before he got her pregnant and, in the event that he couldn't manage *that*, definitely before the child was born."

"Oh, Doug, how can you be such a hypocrite?" his wife admonished with a coy little smile. "Why, as I recall—"

"Never mind," he interjected hastily. "Anything you decide is fine with me."

They chose a late-afternoon ceremony at St. Jude's church, and a dinner reception at the Royal. Elaine agreed to be maid of honor and in early September the three women went shopping for Sophie's wedding dress.

Given the circumstances, Sophie refused to wear white but compromised with a long gown of heavy blush pink satin embroidered with pearls. "Because I know you've been looking forward to this from the minute I was born, Mom," she said.

"And a veil," Anne begged. "Please, Sophie! The gown cries out for a veil, even if it's just one of those short affairs."

"All right, but no train or it'll still be coming in the door when I arrive at the altar. St. Jude's is a very small church, you know."

"Stuffed quail," Anne and Sophie suggested when it came time to choose the dinner menu.

"Roast beef," Doug insisted, and Dominic concurred.

"Actually," he confessed that night, climbing between the sheets and leaning on one elbow to watch Sophie giving the baby his last feeding of the day, "I'd have agreed to stewed truck tires if that's what he'd wanted. Anything to earn a few brownie points with my future father-in-law!"

"He's mellowing by the minute, sweetheart," Sophie said placidly. "After all, you fell in love with me, so you can't be all bad."

"Speaking of which," Dominic said, tracing a possessive fingertip over her lush breast as she propped the baby on her shoulder and patted him on the back, "how much longer do we have to wait before we can make love again?"

She cast a quick glance at the clock on the bedside table. "About five minutes, I'd say—or as long as it takes me to coax a burp out of your son."

For once, Ryan cooperated.

In the weeks that followed, everyone cooperated. Plans meshed with the ease of well-oiled machine parts slipping into place. The long, hot days of summer were forgotten as autumn slipped into winter. By the end of the first week in December, Jewel Lake sparkled under a thin coating of ice.

The Saturday before the wedding, Dominic brought home a nine-foot-tall Noble fir Christmas tree. That evening, he draped it in colored lights while Sophie hung spun-glass balls from its branches. Ryan supervised the entire operation from his swing by the fire, gurgling approval the whole time. Later, with the baby fast asleep in his nursery, they toasted their first Christmas in their new home with champagne and made love on the rug before the fire.

In a passing nod to tradition, Dominic moved back to his penthouse two nights before he was to meet Sophie at the altar. And instead of Sophie going to stay with her parents, they came to stay with her because their place was so small and it was much more convenient.

"I'll miss you," she whispered, snuggling up to Dominic at the front door of their house just before he left. "This'll be the first time we've slept apart since Ryan was born."

He kissed her long and hard. "And the last, if I have my way."

And then, early on the morning of the day before the wedding, it started to snow. At first, it was nothing more than a dusting that settled lightly on the naked branches of the trees, but by midafternoon the view across the lake was obscured behind swirling flakes as big as dimes.

"What if the cars can't make it up the hill to the church?" Sophie's mother fretted, patrolling back and forth in front of the French doors with Ryan in her arms. "What if the airport has to close and Paul and Jenny miss the whole thing?"

"What if the baby throws up in the middle of the service or the groom doesn't show?" Sophie's father replied, dropping a sly wink at his daughter behind her mother's back. "If it's trouble you're looking for, Anne, there's always plenty to be found."

"Sometimes, Doug," Anne snapped, "I wonder why I married you!"

"Because you had to," he said wryly. "As you're so fond of recalling at the most inappropriate times, you were already expecting the twins and I didn't like the way your father's shotgun was aimed at my backside. Hand my grandson to me, for Pete's sake, before you drop him."

"Don't worry about a thing, honey," Dominic told Sophie when he phoned to say good-night. "I picked up Paul and Jenny at the airport half an hour ago, and I've got a crew on standby to clear the roads tomorrow, if necessary. One way or another, I'll get you to the church on time. You're not slipping through my fingers again."

Sophie didn't lose sleep over any of it. She believed in that old adage about the sun shining on happy brides, and her faith was rewarded. By her wedding morning, the skies arched blue and brilliant over Jewel Lake, showing off Palmerstown in all its dazzling glory. Ryan surveyed the world in wide-eyed wonder from his grandfather's arms while Sophie, her mother and Elaine gave each other manicures.

At four o'clock, two long white limousines drew up outside the front door. There was plenty of room in one for all the trappings a baby might need at his first wedding, and for his grandmother and the maid of honor.

Sophie rode in the other with her father. "You know," he said, clasping her hand in both of his, "I wasn't sure Dominic was good enough for you when all this started. But seeing how happy he makes you, and the way you look at each other, well, I have to say I think you've both done pretty well for yourselves, and that grandson of mine is a lucky little guy."

Sophie hadn't thought it was possible for the day to get any better, but this kudo from her hard-to-please father added the finishing touch. "Don't make me cry, Daddy," she said shakily. "You'll ruin my mascara."

St. Jude's, all dressed up for the season, was packed. Scarlet poinsettias lined the steps leading to the altar. In the narthex, where the wedding party took their places to begin the processional, stood a softly backlit Nativity scene with painted figures of the Holy Family kneeling amid straw brought in from one of the nearby farms.

"They're ready for us," Anne said, straightening the collar of Ryan's blue velvet outfit. "I'll take the baby and go to the pew now."

"And here's your bouquet, Sophie," Elaine whispered.

But beautiful though the white lilies were that Dominic had ordered for his bride, Sophie couldn't draw her gaze away from the crèche. It was simple and unpretentious, but it moved her so profoundly that she feared her mascara was going to be washed away before she took one step down the aisle and past the guests waiting with such an expectant hush for her to appear.

"Sophe?" Elaine gave her a little nudge. "What's up? You're not getting cold feet at this stage, are you?"

"No, but there's been a last-minute change of plan," she said. "Here, Mom, you take my flowers and walk in with Daddy."

"What? Sophie, you can't come down the aisle empty-handed and alone."

"I know," Sophie said, holding out her arms for her son and pressing a kiss to his downy head.

If the guests at the Casson-Winter wedding happened to notice that the mother of the bride carried the bouquet intended for her daughter, they appeared not to care. They were too delighted by the sight of the bride carrying her infant son down the aisle to meet his father at the altar.

"It seemed the right thing to do," Sophie whispered when she reached Dominic's side. "Ryan should be part of this, not just an onlooker. We're a family after all. Do you mind?"

"Mind?" Dominic's voice was suspiciously hoarse. "How could I mind when you look like an angel and a Madonna all rolled into one? Anything you choose to do is fine by me if it makes you happy."

"Knowing you love me and Ryan is all it takes to do that, Dominic," she said.

Dominic reached over and settled his son on his right arm, then placed his left hand firmly around Sophie's sweetly slender waist. "I will love you both for the rest of time, my darling," he promised huskily. "You can count on that."

Happy Birthday to

Harlequin Romance®

It's party time....
This year is our
40th anniversary!

**Forty years of
bringing you the best
in romance fiction—and
the best just keeps
getting better!**

To celebrate, we're planning
three months of fun, and prizes.

Not to mention, of course,
some fabulous books...

The party starts in **April** with:

Betty Neels
Emma Richmond
Kate Denton
Barbara McMahon

Come join the party!

HARLEQUIN®

Don't miss these Harlequin favorites by some of our most distinguished authors!
And now, you can receive a discount by ordering two or more titles!

HT#25645	THREE GROOMS AND A WIFE by JoAnn Ross	$3.25 U.S. $3.75 CAN.	☐
HT#25647	NOT THIS GUY by Glenda Sanders	$3.25 U.S. $3.75 CAN.	☐
HP#11725	THE WRONG KIND OF WIFE by Roberta Leigh	$3.25 U.S. $3.75 CAN.	☐
HP#11755	TIGER EYES by Robyn Donald	$3.25 U.S. $3.75 CAN.	☐
HR#03416	A WIFE IN WAITING by Jessica Steele	$3.25 U.S. $3.75 CAN.	☐
HR#03419	KIT AND THE COWBOY by Rebecca Winters	$3.25 U.S. $3.75 CAN.	☐
HS#70622	KIM & THE COWBOY by Margot Dalton	$3.50 U.S. $3.99 CAN.	☐
HS#70642	MONDAY'S CHILD by Janice Kaiser	$3.75 U.S. $4.25 CAN.	☐
HI#22342	BABY VS. THE BAR by M.J. Rodgers	$3.50 U.S. $3.99 CAN.	☐
HI#22382	SEE ME IN YOUR DREAMS by Patricia Rosemoor	$3.75 U.S. $4.25 CAN.	☐
HAR#16538	KISSED BY THE SEA by Rebecca Flanders	$3.50 U.S. $3.99 CAN.	☐
HAR#16603	MOMMY ON BOARD by Muriel Jensen	$3.50 U.S. $3.99 CAN.	☐
HH#28885	DESERT ROGUE by Erine Yorke	$4.50 U.S. $4.99 CAN.	☐
HH#28911	THE NORMAN'S HEART by Margaret Moore	$4.50 U.S. $4.99 CAN.	☐

(limited quantities available on certain titles)

	AMOUNT	$
DEDUCT:	**10% DISCOUNT FOR 2+ BOOKS**	$
ADD:	**POSTAGE & HANDLING**	$
	($1.00 for one book, 50¢ for each additional)	
	APPLICABLE TAXES*	$_____
	TOTAL PAYABLE	$_____
	(check or money order—please do not send cash)	

To order, complete this form and send it, along with a check or money order for the total above, payable to Harlequin Books, to: **In the U.S.:** 3010 Walden Avenue, P.O. Box 9047, Buffalo, NY 14269-9047; **In Canada:** P.O. Box 613, Fort Erie, Ontario, L2A 5X3.

Name: _____

Address: _____ City: _____

State/Prov.: _____ Zip/Postal Code: _____

*New York residents remit applicable sales taxes.
  Canadian residents remit applicable GST and provincial taxes.
Look us up on-line at: http://www.romance.net

HBACK-JM